Me,
Dead Dad,
& Alcatraz

Me, Dead Dad, & Alcatraz

BY Chris Lynch

HARPERCOLLINSPUBLISHERS

Me, Dead Dad, & Alcatraz

www.harperteen.com

Library of Congress Cataloging-in-Publication Data
Lynch, Chris.
Me, dead Dad, & Alcatraz / Chris Lynch.—1st ed.
p. cm.
Summary: With the arrival of his uncle Alex, who his mother
always said was dead, fourteen-year-old Elvin learns more important truths about his family and himself.
ISBN-10: 0-06-059709-7 — ISBN-10: 0-06-059710-0 (lib. bdg.)
ISBN-13: 978-0-06-059709-2 — ISBN-13: 978-0-06-059710-8
(lib. bdg.)
[1. Uncles—Fiction. 2. Self-perception—Fiction. 3. Conduct
of life—Fiction. 4. Family problems—Fiction.] I. Title: Me,
dead Dad, and Alcatraz. II. Title.
PZ7.L9845Me 2005   2004027673
[Fic]—dc22   CIP
                                                            AC

Typography by Hilary Zarycky
1 2 3 4 5 6 7 8 9 10
❖
First Edition

To EJ,
a Hairy-Handed Gent indeed

Contents

Me,
Dead Dad,
& Alcatraz

1

I Think, Therefore I Am, I Think

Who are you?

How do you figure?

How are you supposed to know anything, really, but specifically, how are you supposed to know who you are?

Who am I, and what am I, and if I think I have worked that out, what happens if something new falls into the gumbo and changes it? Does that make me something new entirely? Should I get new clothes?

I found my mother sitting on the footboard of my bed with her back to me. It was an unsettling thing to wake up to, and I knew she hadn't come to tell me there were no blueberries for my pancakes.

"Elvin, have we ever talked about your father's brother Alex?"

The simple questions are always the worst. If you think you know the answer right off, then for God's sake dive into your laundry hamper. If you're completely lost, you're probably okay.

"Ya. The one who died in the plane crash, right?"

A brief, buzzy silence.

"Oh. So I did say that, then."

Should a mother really have to check and see what she has told you in the past? I'd have to say no.

"Um, ya, you did say that. *Ma*. Because he died. In a plane crash."

Because her back was to me, I was reading her shoulders. They slumped. They slumped and gradually sort of folded forward in a gesture of deceit and shame and awfulness before she finally stood and, keeping her back to me, said, "Except that he didn't, die in a plane crash. He is, more specifically, on the couch having a cup of tea and an English muffin with marmalade. Would you like an English muffin with some marmalade?"

Well then. What does one say?

"Not dead, you say?" is what I said.

Her sorry shoulders shrugged. But at least she turned around to face me. "It was really for your own good, Elvin."

"I know, and I'll understand someday, and I'll thank you when I'm older, and you had always intended to tell me when the time was right, but the time was never right, blah blah—"

"Oh God, no, I was never going to tell if you didn't catch me."

Sometimes her refreshing honesty really bunches me up. Especially when it's woven with great, whopping lies.

All this and I wasn't even out of bed yet. It was a wonder I ever woke up at all. Someday, I figured, I just wouldn't. Possibly tomorrow, if it's not really sunny.

"You know, Ma, stuff like this is the reason I'm fat and mental."

"You are not mental; you're just big boned. Put on your bathrobe, because your uncle is waiting to meet you."

Just the words. Just the thought and the words banged up together like that, about my father having a brother, and his brother having an English muffin. Right downstairs. Waiting for me. Wanting to see me. What could he want from me? I had a ghost uncle, and he was waiting for me. It was like a total Shakespeare tragedy.

And I was no tragic hero.

My uncle. All my father's people were gone, and most of my mother's, apart from a few distant stragglers clinging to the rocks of our family history. I thought we were all we had, and you know, I had gotten okay with us being all we had. I even liked being all we had.

I was told that by my *mother*. You hear something like that from your mother, you have to think you've got it from a fairly reliable source. But that would be *your* mother; this was *my* mother.

So if she made up the plane crash . . . what else wasn't true? How many other dead people were out there roaming the landscape waiting to come sit on our couch? Could I be infested with all kinds of grandparents and cousins and things that I never knew I had and that, frankly, I didn't want?

When something is too much to contemplate, there is only one rational way to go. I would not contemplate it. The story of the plane crash that killed my father's brother Alex was true. It was tragic and romantic and didn't hurt me one little bit. There was no Alex anymore.

"Who are you?" was my icebreaker before I was even all the way down the stairs.

"Hi, Elvin, I'm Alex," he said when I walked through the living room door. He sprinted to me and started pumping my hand wildly. His hand was marmalade sticky.

"No, you're not," I said, pulling my hand back gradually.

The guy turned back toward the couch, where my mother was now sitting with a cup of tea. She shrugged.

"I told you he'd say something like that," she said.

"Why are you letting yourself be conned?" I demanded of my normally fabulously skeptical mother.

"He's a fake. He probably just wants our money."

"We don't have any money, Elvin."

"Really? Still?" the guy said. He had concern, both on his face and in his voice. He was nearly convincing. "Well, maybe I can help you all out with that, too."

"Oh . . . jeez, Ma, look what you did now. You embarrassed us in front of the con man."

"I am not a con man. And you have no reason to be embarrassed in front of me."

As if she heard that as an invitation, or a challenge, or her cue, my dog came slouching into the room. Grog.

"Oh mercy," the guy said. "What have we got here?"

"Grog is what we have here. That's our idea of a dog. So you see, we wouldn't have anything you'd be interested in."

He recovered quickly, and I had to give him points for actually crouching down to pet her. Most people just pull their hands up into their sleeves. "Don't believe I've ever seen a breed like him before. What is he?"

"He's a she, that's what he is."

"No offense, but I think I know a penis when I see one."

"That's not a penis. We're not sure what it is, but we are sure she has had puppies. They're not here anymore. The Smithsonian took most of them, and Roswell has the rest."

5

Still crouching, still politely stroking the hairy slab of mystery meat that was Grog, he turned once more back toward Ma.

"Why is he doing this?"

"Well, he's doing this because this is what Elvin does. But also, he is mostly telling the truth about Grog."

"And you want to know what else," I said, because he was still here, "yesterday afternoon Grog covered the whole family, but mostly me, and not you at all, in glory by getting beat up by another dog, not just any dog, but a tiny dog wearing a tiny tartan rain jacket."

I had, of course, seen pictures of my father, though not many, and not lately, and not easily. And not only did this stranger fail to not look like my father, he failed to not make my funny and gabby mother stare at him in near silence and even nearer awe, whenever he wasn't looking.

"So you see, stranger," I said, "there is danger here. You'd probably better be on your way before I turn the beast loose on you. He only lives next door. He can have his jacket on in a second and be over here."

He stood up. The guy stood up, the stranger, after giving Grog a last extra-scratchy shake of her big, unnatural head, and he talked to me serious and warm and not bothered by my stuff.

"Maybe I could help you out, with training up the dog

a bit. Maybe I could help with a few things. I would like to do that, help out. I came here to help, Elvin Bishop."

"Whoever he is, he's not here to help. I don't care if he is out buying blueberries."

"He is not buying blueberries; stop talking about blueberries. He's taking a walk around the block because I asked him to so I can try and stabilize you. Who he is, Elvin, is your uncle. Alex really is your late father's brother."

I sipped my tea. I took a bite of my muffin. I do not like marmalade. There is a reason people compost orange peels.

"I guess you have some explaining to do," I said.

"I guess I do. I told you Alex was dead, because that was what Alex wanted."

"Why would he want that? Was he so ashamed people would know we were related that he needed to play dead about it?"

"No, no, nothing like that at all. In fact, it wasn't us he was ashamed of, but himself. Your uncle Alex did some pretty lousy things, back when."

I sat up straight on the couch and stopped chewing. "He did?"

Here's a thing. When I heard my mother say my uncle did some bad stuff, something clicked. Something not altogether unpleasant. I ever so slightly liked him better for a second, or liked the *idea* of him better, even if he scared me more at the same time. I felt the tiniest little babbling stream of badness running through my blood, my bloodline, and I wanted to know more about it.

Or maybe it was simply the rush of suddenly *having* a bloodline to learn more about, with the bonus that it was not a boring bloodline.

"Did he kill somebody?"

"Of course he didn't kill somebody. Do you think I would have a killer in this house, Elvin?"

"You? I don't know what you're capable of at all. Maybe he is a killer. Maybe you're a killer. You did kill my uncle before bringing him back to life. I don't think I know you at all anymore, that's what I think. Who are you, lady?"

She listened, lips pinched tight together, until I ran out of stuff. Then she went to the kitchen and came back with a fresh cup of tea for herself and a blue ceramic saucer with orange segments fanned around the perimeter. She never leaves any of those white veins on the surface of the orange, which is pretty great, whoever she is.

"Right," she said. "He didn't kill anybody."

"Hijackings? Kidnappings?"

"No." Sip of tea. "No." Orange segment. "Want one?"

"Yes, please. Gunrunning? Smuggling? Did my uncle topple a government?"

"Steady, boy. Alex didn't do anything like that. He was guilty of . . . indiscretions."

I stared at her. Grog stared at me. The dog wanted the slice of orange I was holding. I wanted a meatier answer.

I passed on my fruit to my dog, hoping that maybe karma would then dictate I got what I wanted.

It was not, by a very long shot, the first time karma shortchanged me.

"Ma?" I made the come-here hand gestures like I was helping her back up a truck. "Indiscretions? What're indiscretions? I am guilty of indiscretions. Grog is guilty of indiscretions. But bringing a doggy bag to an all-you-can-eat restaurant is not something you want to be erased from history for, and neither is getting a hedgehog stuck to your nose. So what is the deal here?"

She sighed sadly, very sadly, a sad sigh that floated out of her and seeped into me. "It was a long time ago, Elvin," she said. "Alex is a sensitive man." Sighed again, seeped again, deeper. "Like your dad was. Like you are."

"I am not—"

"When he wanted to be dead rather than telling you about his mistakes, he meant it. He meant it so much that when I first refused to lie, he told me he would then make it so I didn't have to lie. Do you hear, Elvin, what I'm telling you?"

Was I sensitive, really? Was that what I was?

"I do. I hear you."

Sensitive. You couldn't look like me, and act like me, and then be all touchy about it afterward. It just wouldn't work. I was not sensitive.

"Then you should understand that Alex should be allowed to keep some details to himself. There may come a time when you'll need to know more, but please just appreciate that now is not that time."

Even the term bothered me. *Sensitive.* Just the word itself was some kind of insult, some kind of implied accusation that you were too much of a lot of the wrong things. Too soft, too weak, too lame to even exist. I was not sensitive. *Sensitive* was code for *pathetic.* I had a good many flaws, but I was not in any way sensitive, and my mother really hurt my feelings by suggesting that I was. Sensitive, hell.

"I am not sensitive. Don't say that again."

I perhaps had spent too much time thinking there before speaking. Because by the time I spoke, my mother had finished her tea and Alex had finished his walk around the block and was rapping his sensitive knuckles on the door.

Ma stared at me. "Sorry, son. Did I say *sensitive*? I

meant self-absorbed." She was at the door, hand on the doorknob. "Remember, easy does it," she warned.

"Are you kidding? I am Mr. Easy Does It. I have a tattoo that says that. I'll leave him his mysteries, since he's so sensitive, like me."

She pulled open the door and there he was, standing in the beginnings of a rain that kinked up his hair like the fibers of a thick, cheap, synthetic, rust-colored rug. Which he may, in fact, have been wearing.

"Hey," he said with a wobbly, shame-drenched grin. "So did you tell him how I stole all that money from you and all?"

2

Blood Type E

"No, I'm not kidding. He is an actual blood relative."

"I thought you didn't have any actual blood relatives except for your mother."

"That's what I thought. I was wrong."

"Well, great. That's great, Elvin."

Frankie and I were standing in my living room, hovering over the sleeping body of my new uncle Alex. Ma was out doing the shopping. The shopping according to the list drawn up by my new uncle Alex. Because it turned out that in addition to being a gifted thief and undead, he was allegedly something of a chef. He even insisted on paying for all the groceries with his own money. Well, somebody's own money, but at least it wasn't ours.

A chef. If he was merely trying to worm his way into this house for some nefarious purpose, he had at least done his homework.

"Is that a rug he's wearing?" Frankie wanted to know. He leaned way down close to examine Alex's suspicious-looking hairline. "Because a criminal I could maybe overlook . . . but if his head looks this nasty by *choice*, I think we maybe have bigger problems."

Frankie was very serious about hair. Hair as a barometer of practically everything.

"And where does that come from, the hair issues? Mother's side or father's?"

"I don't know. Jeez, Frank, don't you think there are other things here that—"

"I would care if I were you. I would care very much. That could be your future, lying underneath this mess."

Now he made me curious. I inched up next to him. We were both on the verge of touching it, of lifting a corner. . . .

When I came to my senses a little, and pulled him away.

He stood shaking his head. "If I were you, El, I'd be hoping that was a rug. I wouldn't want hair like that anywhere near my bloodline."

There, you see. You see what happens? A very short time ago, I had no bloodline. Life was simple and good, and now . . . now I had to start figuring everything out all over again.

Lots of guys I knew worried about all these things. They would look at their fathers and their uncles and their grandfathers, and they would worry about what life-tricks were going to be played on them when they got older. Yes, ignorance is bliss, and I *like* bliss.

Well, I had fewer worries than most guys, right? Because I didn't have the blueprint, the bloodline. I had me, and my blood, Type E, and while there were bound to be flaws aplenty in that DNA, the beauty of it was in the one thing I could do about it.

I could believe what I wanted to believe. And if my mother had any extra bits of crummy old reality she needed to get off her chest every once in a while, I had two stout index fingers that fit exactly the diameter of my earholes. That, to me, was evolution at its most cunning best.

But now I had this. Darwin's big ape showing up and flopping right down in front of me on my own couch—here, I feared, to say stuff I never asked to hear.

"I hear you're a creative type," Alex said without opening his eyes, causing Frankie and me to both jump back and mill in a circle like you do when there's a fight or something and you want to pretend like you weren't doing anything. Even though we weren't doing anything.

"Who said that?" I said. "I am no such thing. Who told you that? They're lying."

"What's the big deal? Your mother just mentioned—"

"Don't ever listen to her. She gets bored, and she makes stuff up. Usually about me. She's always trying to make me sound like this weird character."

Another thing my mother had apparently told him was how to deal with me by ignoring when I rant.

"Hi," Alex said, popping up off the couch and shaking Frankie's hand. "I'm Alex. Elvin's uncle."

"Hi," Frank said.

"By the way, this is my real hair," Alex said, smiling. "I wouldn't care what my head looked like; I'd never wear any rug. A guy looks ten times more ridiculous with one of those things on his head than with a regular shiny dome. You play with the gear God gave you, is what you do."

"Well . . . okay," Frank said. He was a little thrown, with the sudden live and kicking Alex, and it showed.

"Jeez, don't you worry," Alex said, as if this were the problem, as if looks and self-confidence were ever Frankie's problem or ever likely to be. "Your equipment's great. You got beautiful equipment. My Lord, this is one beautiful man. Elvin, this is a majorly handsome friend you got here, you know that? Are there any girls left over at all for any of the rest of you with this guy around?"

First, because I didn't know Alex yet, I couldn't tell how much was serious in there and how much was teasing. Second, because I didn't know Alex yet, I couldn't even tell if these were actual questions that were supposed to be answered. And from his silence, neither did Frank.

Until Alex whirled around, smiling broadly at me, and poked me—harpooned me—right in the belly with an abnormally long and sharp index finger.

"Ow," I said.

But he was the one who looked stunned. "I practically lost my whole arm in there, Elvin. That tummy of yours didn't offer any resistance at all. Here, tighten up this time."

"Ow," I said.

"Whoa. Nephew, I hope you don't mind my saying so, but you could use a little work. I think maybe I showed up just in time."

It was my great fortune to have Frank recover his composure and his sense of humor at this point.

"Well, I don't know about just in time. I think maybe three or four years ago would have been just in time."

"Thanks, pal, you can be quiet now."

"Not to worry, not to worry," Alex assured me. "We can fix you."

Fix me. "Fix me?" Fix me. I was not to worry, because we could fix me. Sounded pretty worrying to me, actually.

"Sure. We can work on you, have you as dashing and strapping as your movie star friend here."

And this is how stupid and weak and pathetic people can be. Well, me anyway. I did a double take. Dashing and strapping. I gave it thought. Serious thought. I let this seem important and good.

I thought about the possibility that I could look like Frankie. That had never been suggested by anyone out loud before. Be like Frankie. That, well, that would be something. That, I had to admit, would be a dream come true. A dream of many years' standing come true. Frankie, frankly, was the most handsome, and therefore luckiest and most successful and most self-confident, guy in the world. Nobody would not want to be Frankie, because God gave Frankie *everything*.

Oh right. Almost forgot. God.

God given.

Alex wasn't really here to tell me I was like Frankie. He was here to tell me I was like *him*. It was in the blood.

"I don't know, El," Frankie said. He was at the mirror in my bedroom. He was staring at himself. I was staring at himself. He started brushing his hair, which was not unusual. He had great hair. Auburn, longish, curly but not big curly, soft. It had a shine, and would catch any little bits of light, like the crystal drops off a chandelier, and flash them back in your face wherever you were to remind you, hey, I'm Frankie's hair. It was no wonder he was brushing it all the time. I would brush it all the time if it were my hair. I think I'd brush it anyway, if he'd let me.

"What don't you know, Frank?"

"About your uncle. I mean, he's probably cool and everything, but I don't know about that hair. You can tell lots about a guy by his hair, and that's very suspicious hair he has there."

"Well, of course." Well, of course. Look at Frankie's hair. "Look at your hair. Everybody's hair looks like crap next to your hair." Except Alex's hair really was in a whole different category. It was thin, sort of, though there were no bald spots. It didn't move. It was wiry, but it wasn't curly. It was like water, in that it didn't seem to be parted anywhere or brushed in one way or another, not forward or back, not side parted and not middle. It was all texture. Stucco? Holly bush? And the color was something not found in nature. If you crossed, say, olive with peach, you'd be in the ballpark.

"Ya, but I'm not comparing his hair to my hair. That would be unfair. I'm comparing . . ."

He went on talking, and brushing, and looking at himself. But I was distracted. All of a sudden my ability to hear went haywire as my other senses became overloaded and mish-mushed. It was a combined assault of things that shouldn't really be having anything to do with each other.

I was smelling stuff. Food stuff, coming up the stairs from the kitchen, where my uncle was apparently making good on his claim to be a megachef. Spices and meats and sauces and starches, in mixtures foreign to me, were pulling at me like two fingers hooked into my nostrils and yanking me toward the kitchen.

And at the same time, I was staring, at Frankie. Staring, I mean staring-staring. I watched his hair as he brushed it over and over and over again. It got softer with every stroke. It got shinier with every stroke, and . . .

Lamb. There was definitely some lamb going on down there. And something pork related, and something saffron . . .

He switched hands and started brushing the left side of his head with the left hand, in order to get the same symmetrical strokage happening all over, and thereby achieve that almost unnatural unity of hair. Genius hair, it was.

It was sweet now, the aroma. No. Spicy. Oh, both together. Pungent. Rich. Very glutinous rice was being mixed with something fruity. I am not too proud to admit I was salivating. My mouth was filling like a bathtub.

He was shaking his head now. Making the curls jump. Jump, you curls. They jumped. They settled down again. One landed out of place. Frankie raised a hand and brought it across his brow to adjust the one wayward, glowing, lock of—

"What are you doing?" he asked, startlingly enough to make me turn away and scuttle for the door like a thief.

"Where are you going, Elvin?"

"I was not staring at your hair."

I walked right into Mikie.

"Yes, you were," Mike said. "I didn't see it, but you were. You're always staring at his hair."

"That's not true," Frankie said, coming surprisingly to my defense. "Sometimes he stares at my eyes," he added, less surprisingly.

"Hey, shut up," I said.

"Calm down," Frank said. "I don't mind. At least it shows you have good taste. It just gets a little spooky when it goes on too long."

"Shut up. It doesn't go on too long."

"What are you so upset about?" Mike asked. "It couldn't be Frankie's hair; that looks like it always does. What's wrong?"

Finally.

I opened my mouth to state my case. My case failed to emerge.

I didn't know what I was upset about.

"It's his uncle's hair," Frank said. "He's afraid, now that he's met his uncle, that he's going to turn out like his uncle because his uncle is practically like his dad."

"I never said that—"

Mikie interrupted. "The hair is a maternal issue, isn't it? Doesn't it come from the mother's side of the family?"

If this in fact was not my problem, why did I react like this . . . ?

"Really? Is that true? God, you're the best. You usually know what you're talking about, Mike, so it must be true that I won't get hair like Alex, right? If it's maternal issues you're talking about, I'm your man, right? No bigger mama's boy than me."

"Well," Frank said, addressing his reflection as if the two of them were the only two beings in the room and this was a serious academic discussion about an issue of global importance, "I know hair. And I know people say that about the hair coming from the mother's side, but I don't buy it. How many guys have you seen whose heads look exactly like their old man's head? Look at that guy Chuckie, on the basketball team, and his father the coach. Slapheads, the pair of them."

"Ah, you could be right there, Franko. Now that you mention it—"

"Shut up," I snapped. This was bothering me *so* much, especially after it was only minutes ago that I had been drifting away on a cloud of juicy meats and spices and the hypnotic rhythm of Frank brushing, brushing. . . .

"Hey, don't yell at me," Mike said. "You're the guy who's so obsessed by everybody's hair. Anyway, I met your uncle on my way in. Seems nice enough. But instead of the hair, I would think there would be a lot more pressing stuff to worry about. Why's he here? Where's he been? And what was the big hoo-ha you couldn't tell me about on the phone?"

"He stole all Elvin's money," Frank said.

Then the three of us migrated together toward my bed and sat there, side by side by side.

"Did he steal from you, El?"

"Well, not right out of my pocket, no."

"Out of his trust fund."

"You had a trust fund?"

"Can you believe it, Mikie? All this time we've been hanging around with a Rockefeller baby and we didn't even know—"

"Would you let me tell this?"

"Sorry."

"My father left some money. For me and my mother. But he put Alex in charge of it."

"Why did he do that?"

"Because Alex is a money guy. Or at least he was, before they took away his money-guy license or whatever it is they do when you don't do it very honorably. He did people's taxes, and managed their finances, and made, you know, investments for them. That was his job."

"His other job was horse races and casinos."

"Franko . . ."

"Sorry."

"So what's the real story then?"

I didn't get a chance to make it sound less awful.

"That was the real story," Alex said from the doorway. We all whipped our heads in that direction to find Alex there, leaning and smiling and frowning at once. "My brother was dying, and he asked me to take care of money matters for his son and his wife. Then he went and died. My sister-in-law, the widow Bishop, trusted me to do a good job. I stole her money and lost every bit of it. And I stole her little boy's money, that boy right there, and I lost every bit of that."

I turned away from Alex, because I didn't like this whatsoever, and couldn't take it. Now I could see the side of Mike's head in the mirror as he looked at Alex, and I could see Frank face on, since he had already gone back to looking at himself. They were both riveted.

"And so now I am here," Alex said, "seeking redemption. From the only people who can offer it to me. Come on downstairs. Supper is ready."

There was almost a whoosh sound, as Alex left a big empty in his wake.

Mike continued staring after him for several seconds.

"Whoa," said Mikie.

"I hope I don't have too many more relatives I don't know about," I said.

Frankie stood up. "We better get down there. God knows what he'll do if we're late for supper."

"Holy smokes," I said as I led the small procession to the dining room table. I said *holy smokes* for the traditional shock expression that it was, but also for the fact that the whole room seemed to be smoking. Not that it was filled with smoke itself, but like the room was smoked, barbecue, hickory smoked. I wanted to eat the walls.

Ma was already seated, and Alex marched into the room and pointed at individual chairs with his ladle, indicating where the rest of us were to sit.

"There, there, and there," he said before disappearing back into the kitchen.

"What are we having?" I asked Ma as I took my seat next to her. I was at one end of the table, with her on my right, the guys to my left, and Alex's empty place staring straight at me from the opposite end seat.

"I don't know," Ma said. "He wouldn't let me help, or even see. I know the ingredients, but not what he did with them, exactly. I do know he used the microwave a lot, and the broiler and the stove top. The place was as steamy as a bathhouse, only you wanted to eat the vapors with a spoon. Since he wouldn't let me do anything, I just sat here absorbing it. I've been sitting right here in this seat for the last hour, closing my eyes and lapping it up."

She was describing an exact dream I had had over and over.

"You told," Alex said as he walked through the door again with two bowls in his hands.

"I didn't tell anything," she said.

"I hope you didn't spoil it." He plunked the bowls in front of Ma and Frankie, then came back with two more, plunked one down in front of Mikie's place, and then his own. Everybody was served but me, even the guy who wasn't here yet.

Then he came in with mine, setting down a heaving, hissing bowl of the most intense soup I had ever sat in front of.

"Dig in, everyone," Alex said. "It's a little thrown together, I'm afraid, a little rushed. But it's based on callaloo soup, something I found during my time living in Jamaica. I hope you like it."

"You lived in Jamaica?" Ma asked.

Alex just nodded, then scooped a big load of soup into his mouth, watching to see that everyone did likewise.

And it was incredible. The soup seemed to have a

thousand flavors going at once. There was some crab in there, some haddock, big chunks of chicken and little ones of bacon. I recognized my old pal garlic there, and his buddy onion. And then it all became murky. I couldn't tell what more was going on because I couldn't slow down enough to work it out, but much more was going on.

The crowd was unanimous about the soup. Everybody slurped and made those moaning, semiword sounds as they thanked and praised the chef without insulting him by slowing down.

Until I did. There were big glasses of water in front of each of us, and a pitcher in the middle of the table, and good thing, too, because as I passed the halfway mark of my bowl, there was a cumulative effect coming on. It was getting hot.

Quite hot.

I put down my soup spoon and took up my glass. Drank half the water down, cooling the heat. I put down my glass, surveyed the crowd to find everyone eating comfortably, then picked up my own spoon again.

Then put it down again.

I finished my glass of water, poured another, then drank half of that.

"Are you all right, Elvin?" Ma asked.

"Sure," I said. "Kind of hot. Fine, though."

Alex laughed, like we were sharing a joke. "Oh ya, me

and your dad, we always liked the hottest stuff. Especially your dad. I'd be on the floor crying from some chillies he found in Mexico on vacation, while he'd be chewing on them like they were gum and laughing like crazy. It was something, I wanna tell ya. I thought maybe you had the taste like the old man so, ya, yours and my soup's maybe a little feistier than the rest. I could take it back, though, Elvin, because I am very sorry if it's not what—"

"No," I said, the last sips of water already evaporating with the heat. "No way, don't you touch my soup. I love feisty. I can't get enough feisty."

"Really?" Ma said.

"Really?" Mikie said.

"What's the big deal?" Frank asked, yet again surprising me by coming to my aid. "The guy'll eat anything." And still, I don't know *why* I kept being surprised.

Regardless, I was going to finish my soup. It wasn't that spicy anyway, the way really obvious foods burn your tongue right away. This was smoother, subtler, more sophisticated cuisine here, and I loved it. I could see why my dad would have loved it.

"Pass the water please."

"Tell us about Jamaica, Alex?" Frank asked.

"Jamaica," Alex said as he stood, after he'd tipped up his bowl and emptied the contents into his wide mouth, "is hot. Great food. Great spices, great music. It is true that the hotter the climate, the hotter the food, and the closer I have ever come to the equator, the more singed I got." He went around collecting bowls. "As you will see in a minute, when you taste my jeweled rice from Iran, to go alongside my own concoction, Vietnamese chilli-roast chicken-lamb burgers."

"Oh my God," I burped. I actually burped the words. I achieved something else with that sentence: I expressed two 100 percent contradictory feelings at once and completely meant them both. *Oh my God*, that sounded like fantastic food, and I was already opening extra salivary glands to handle the rush, and *Oh my God*, more spice when my own saliva was already beginning to burn me.

I was also last finishing my starter, and told Alex to take the other bowls while I finished.

"You sure?" he asked quietly, a look of concern on his face. "You don't need to finish, Elvin. I won't be insulted. You already ate most of it."

"I'm sure," I said gently, whisps of flame escaping through my nostrils.

He left and came back with plates stacked expertly on each arm like a pro waiter. He served all around to more gasps of appreciation.

As he circled around to my end of the table, I gasped as well, though it was a different sort of thing.

But I finished. In Alex's own style—and probably my dead dad's—I tipped up the bowl and emptied the hissing remains down my gullet with a flourish. As I handed over my bowl, I made a loud *ahhh* sound that could have been interpreted a number of ways.

"Well done," Alex said with a big, beaming smile. "I guess you liked it. You might be your father's boy after all."

These are the moments. These are the moments that cause me trouble. I believe I have a fully functional if sometimes hi-de-hee kind of a mind, but really the times when I have caused myself the most problems have been the times when I let some small emotional stimulus enter the situation and cause my heart and my mouth to huddle together on a plan and leave my mind completely out of it.

"Oh, the soup was excellent," I said. "But to tell the truth, I usually like my food *spicy*."

I smiled up at my uncle as broadly as he smiled down at me. I don't know what he thought, with my forehead and upper lip sweating away before him, but I wanted to slap all my teeth out.

"Weh-hell," Alex said, shaking his head, "this train's a-comin' atcha, boy," and he rushed excitedly toward the kitchen, but not before poking me in the stomach with his finger.

* * *

"I don't know exactly what redemption is," Frankie said as he pushed himself back from the table and patted his stomach, which still looked sickeningly flat to me, "but I vote for you to get it, just for the food."

Alex rumbled out a hearty laugh, but looked down at his plate and picked at his pie with his fork.

"You don't get a vote, Frank," said Mikie. "But ya, Alex, your food is really great, man."

"Thank you," he said, still not looking up.

I took a sip of my tea. Chai tea. Even that was spicy. It went over my tongue like it was trying to claw its way back up as I swallowed. My shirt was soaked in sweat. My underwear was soaked in sweat. My socks were soaked in sweat. I was kind of sweaty. I had been to the bathroom three times already as my body processed about seventy-eight spices and seeds and colors it didn't recognize. I ate a large meal and lost weight.

But I did it. I felt good. Well, not physically good. But good.

"Thank you, Alex, that was truly superb," Ma said.

"Ah," Alex said, waving his hand.

Mike and Frank got up to go. They said their thank you's and see ya's and all and made their way to the door, where I should have seen them out. I wasn't really up to it, so fortunately Ma's manners took over for me.

Anyway, I wanted to stay where I was.

We sat directly across from each other, at the opposite ends of the rectangular table. I stared at the top of his head while he stared at his plate.

"What if I decide I don't want to give it to you? What you came for."

He looked up. He smiled hard again, even though he appeared not to want to.

"Your father could be a real difficult piece of work too."

I wished he would stop that. "Stop that. Maybe I'll just say no. What then?"

"You know, Elvin, it's a funny notion, redemption. I'm not even entirely sure you can say no to me. Even if you want to. Not sure if a person can decide to give it or not give it. All I know is, I need it. And it involves you. So we'll see how it goes."

Alex and I just looked and looked at each other then. I was trying to see stuff, as much stuff as it was possible to see in a person from the other end of a table, but that was probably just stupid. He was looking into me, though, and I couldn't help but feel he was doing the better job of it, getting more out of it. I thought for a second he might cry from the look of him, and I started sweating madly again after I had just cooled down.

"You are a very good cook," I blurted just as I heard

my mother shut the front door.

"Thank you," he said. "I am sorry, Elvin. I'm gonna fix everything."

"Everything's not broken. Don't bother."

3

The Devil's Haircut

Like most people, I sweat buckets on the average day. But this sweat was something special. I woke up sweating. Five times. I changed my T-shirt three of them. Felt like I was sleeping on a slick sheet of plastic, which I probably should have done.

When I finally got up for good, I went to the mirror and saw a wreck. Not the wreck I usually found there either. This one was pasty faced and sunken eyed from under-sleep.

And worse, much worse. The hair. My God, the hair. It was as if my head was soaked overnight in a teriyaki marinade, then baked in a clay oven, the result being metallic, yet frayed at the same time like one of those World War II army helmets with the netting on top.

How did he do it? This was an evil genius like I had never encountered, and I had encountered most of them. Somehow my mad uncle had concocted spicy potion food that not only burned me top and tail, but miraculously turned my boring but normal hair into his own rusted ragtop overnight.

"No," I said to my reflection, which stared back at me from the very spot where Frankie's perfect mug had floated just a day earlier. "No, no. Do I not have enough handicaps already? Isn't it just shooting fish in a barrel, to make me socially untouchable? Well then, come on, Lord, work me over; it is your day, after all . . . so do bring it on. Why not give me a couple extra legs, or maybe move my butt to my forehead."

"I couldn't help but hear. . . ," came the unwelcome voice from the other side of my door.

But of course.

"Oh, so you're still around. I thought maybe your work was done here."

"Nah. My work is just starting. And from the sound of the blaspheming I'm hearing from in there, it may take more than I'd imagined."

Uh-oh.

"Could you repeat that please?"

"What, that my work was just beginning?"

"No. The other part."

"About your Sunday morning blasphemy?"

"Mmm-hmm, that's the one. Thanks."

I decided to address this latest development in the great test that was Alex in the way I address most things.

I huddled silently in my bedroom, hoping he would just go away.

"Well, if you want to talk about it, I'll be around," said Alex after an impressive seven silent minutes.

But I did not want to talk about it, my blasphemy, or any other *it*. I didn't want to even see Alex when I got out there, and now I was sentenced to seeing him anyway, in my own mirror.

I had thought about it through the night, through the sweating and changing, through the toilet visits, through the rolling around in bed looking for sleep, finding sleep, then wanting to lose it again because of the dreams. I had thought about my new life here, the one my uncle Alex hauled through the door just yesterday when he stepped back in out of the netherworld of his fake death.

It worried me, I had to say. It made me think about what I was happy enough not to think about for a long time. *It* was staring at me now, out of my own mirror, looking less like me than yesterday, looking more like my uncle, who looked much like my dead dead father.

It made me, as many things do, afraid. But unlike most of those things, the scary stuff Alex brought was possibly stuff that already had my name on it.

So did I have to take delivery?

"Ma, I'm going out," I called loudly as I slid open my bedroom window.

"Elvin," she called from downstairs. "Out *where*? What are you doing?" She sounded a bit worried, which she usually manages not to be despite my behavior.

I was a little worried myself. It wasn't a huge way down, but my view from my bedroom window looking straight down to the patchy lawn below looked like a paratrooper's training exercise. Not only had I not ever tried going out that window even in my devil-may-care younger days, I couldn't ever remember opening the thing wide enough to accommodate my head in these devil-cares-very-much-indeed more mature years. I knew my abilities, and this amounted to a suicide attempt.

So I was forced to retreat and run the gauntlet of the stairs.

"What am I doing? What are *you* doing?" I insisted when I found Alex and my mother dressed up for something and ready to go out. On a Sunday, well before two P.M.

"We're going to church," my mother said.

When I was a kid I had this tic where when someone would say something to me that I found incomprehensible, I would repeat all their words in my head and make it all the more noticeable by moving my lips like a five-year-old ventriloquist with an imaginary dummy.

We're going to church. . . .

"What's that he's doing?" Alex asked my mother as if I couldn't be spoken to directly.

"Stop that, Elvin," she said. "And what is that you've done to your head?"

"I didn't do anything to my head," I said, feebly trying to cover the whole mess with one hand while pointing my accusation finger at the true culprit. "He did."

"What did I do?" Alex asked, almost giggling.

"Elvin, for goodness' sake," Ma said, quite definitely giggling, "what could Alex have done to your hair?"

"I don't know. But it had something to do with the food. My body has been acting very strangely. . . ."

She giggled more.

"And then I woke up with hair . . . like *his*," I said with the conviction of a big TV detective who had uncovered the murderer no one else could uncover because the crime was so insanely complicated and implausible.

"Why are the pretty ones always crazy?" Ma asked the air. Not for the first time.

But because she was a veteran of my stories and my style, she didn't bother trying to work out my logic but did tip a glance toward Alex.

And she started giggling all the harder.

"My God, that's what it is. It is the same hair."

I thought she was having a very good time for some-body who was going to church. Alex smiled indulgently, but didn't seem to be having quite as much fun. Me, I thought my mother was taking a very serious issue way too lightly.

"We kind of thought you might like to come along," Alex said.

"I don't usually. . . ," I said.

"So, neither do I," Ma said. "But I thought it might be nice, for a change."

"You know I don't like change, Mother," I said sternly enough to straighten her out, but not enough to frighten her.

"Oh God, no, not Elvin," she burbled, warmly tugging at Alex's sleeve. She was finding me irresistibly amusing with him here, like somebody who had been waiting ages to tell all her old jokes to somebody who hadn't heard them yet. "He wouldn't change his underwear if I didn't make him."

That was patently untrue.

"I'm sure that's not true," said Alex. "But change can be a very good thing, Elvin," he added alarmingly.

"So," I said in nonresponse, "you're a Jesus guy then?"

Ma switched quickly from her airy voice to her growl-sigh. As a guy in a peanut butter helmet, what did I care?

"Sure," Alex said confidently. "Jesus is a friend of mine."

"And so you're going to introduce your friend to my mother."

"Alex," Ma said, tugging him toward the door, "you don't have to hang around to be grilled by my impolite son. We'll be late."

"No, that's okay. Elvin, you are a sharp, inquisitive boy. Healthily skeptical. I admire that no end. Like your father."

I was still trying to figure out how I felt about that. I zip-banged in every direction whenever he said that about me and my father, but I could not for the life of me tell you whether it was a good or a bad feeling. Only that it was a big, fast, shake of a feeling.

"I like Jesus, and Jesus likes me; that's a fact. It's a relationship we both keep in perspective, though, if you know what I mean."

Of course I did not know what he meant.

Ma opened the front door, blew me a kiss, and headed out. Alex pulled a tweed cap off the coatrack and mercifully covered his head. I stood there, making sure to look him in the eye because that seemed somehow important, even though I was still a little off balance about things.

A relationship we both keep in perspective, if you know what I mean.

He came back and patted me on the cheek. His hand

was very warm. "That's right, keep repeating it. You'll work it out."

"Keep repeating what?"

"We'll talk later, okay?" he said. "Just you and me. About stuff. About everything. You can grill me all you want. And maybe I can grill you." As he said the last bit, he did the thing, backing away and sticking me with one more poke in the belly.

"If you do that one more time. . . ," I growled.

Right, *growled.* I didn't sound anything like myself. I kind of scared and impressed myself.

He grinned hard, and for the first time I noticed he was missing most of the teeth along the right side of his mouth.

Grilling Alex didn't sound like a bad idea at all. Who was he, poking me in the belly all the time? I knew I was a little portly. But that was my issue. I didn't need any reminders, and I didn't need any help, either.

Why was I such a lightning rod for people wanting to improve me all the time? Was I so offensive that people had to come back from the dead to try and fix me up for the greater good of this world *and* the next?

Anyway, who was he? Just because he was skinny, he could offer me tips on living? Because he was skinny and because he used to be related to my dad who used to be alive and used, also, to be related to me? And because he was also good buddies with God?

I happened to be good buddies with God. I was cool with God and God was cool with me. I know, there was the issue of my good buddy's kind of cruel sense of humor, but from my experience a friend is no friend if he cannot dig the needle into you on a regular basis. Like this:

Me: Mikie, I don't know what it is, but I am eating like a horse lately.
Mikie: Like a horse a *day,* from the looks of it, El.

Mikie, as in my best earthly friend, said that. But that was okay, because my next-best earthly friend was right there to jump in. Watch:

Me: I don't care. I have decided to live with it and embrace my inner fat guy.
Frankie: That'll come in handy, El, 'cause I don't think anybody's gonna embrace the outer one.

So there, you see, was my frame of friendship reference. That's what friends did. Therefore, I think I was one up on most people in being able to perceive the Almighty, because while most folks went flailing around and chasing signs and worshipping crying statues and ooohing and ahhhing at stigmata and the like, I knew profoundly that God loved me because he mocked me. I, in turn, praised him by being his straight man. That is why I was not required to go to church or confession or anything else. God and I had a more intimate thing, based on humor. And that, I could understand.

But I didn't have to like it all the time.

"Ahhh," I shrieked as I caught sight of myself in a big plate-glass bakery window. You know that morning bakery smell when all the different stuffs, the various bagels and birthday cakes and muffins and donuts and breads and rolls and danishes and baklava and cannoli and apple pie and blueberry pie and strawberry rhubarb pie and cherry custard tarts are all firing up at the same time and all become one unbelievable, inseparable, satanic, majestic smell?

Right, well, I didn't shriek, exactly, but I did take in a sharp breath of air that made a sound. I had lost myself in the bakery scent and stood there gawping at the window like a cross between a Norman Rockwell scene of wholesomeness in which I would eventually be handed a cruller by a kindhearted baker, and a Grimm fairy tale where a long, twisted, gnarly hand would instead reach out and yank me into an Elvin potpie.

I didn't look too good. I was showing the signs of lack

of sleep, of a poorly chosen T-shirt that had fit me a couple years earlier when Bart Simpson might possibly have still said "Cowabunga" like he was now on my belly, and of the mysterious madness that still swirled on my head. I forgot, I was out to get a haircut.

Peeling away from the bakery window, I assured myself that all that was required here was the proper styling. I had seen the shampoo and conditioner ads. A snip here, a flip there, and you achieved a new confidence that changed everything, put a bounce in your step and removed it from your belly.

Not to mention putting a little distance between your look and your uncle's.

I must have wanted this bad, to go out looking randomly on a Sunday for a haircut. Sal, my regular barber, was closed on Sundays, but I suppose that was part of the plan. I didn't want my regular barber. Not because I normally only went to him because I had done so all my life and he was three doors down from us. Not because he was well past retirement and I had to wake him up sometimes and when I did he usually couldn't find his glasses and then he usually just went ahead with the job anyway. Not because I sometimes went in and got a haircut without needing one just because I was passing his window and he was very alone and wide awake and he waved at me like he was my grandpa and happy to see me. And not because he still gave me lemon or root beer lollipops in the clear wrappers that I don't think you could get without going to an old barber.

I didn't want to go to Sal because he always made me look like me. I didn't want that.

Without much to go on, I cruised the streets of town, finding that there were not only an alarming number of hairdressers, but that most of them were open on Sunday. I thought about going into one and panicked, then walked the whole route again to casually look the whole bunch up and down again.

I didn't know what to look for. It could be hard to tell whether they did guys, for example, although I supposed that in the twenty-first century, everybody probably did. I couldn't take a chance. I decided to consider only the ones that said "Unisex" right there in the window, and had guy pictures alongside all the girls, *and* the guy pictures could not be prettier than the girl pictures. This whittled down the field surprisingly quickly.

Then I eliminated the one where my mother went. And the three others on the same street. Then I crossed off the ones where the hairdressers themselves had scary, large, dry, white and/or sparkly hairstyles. Why would a place that wants your hair business show you atrocities like that if they had the first clue of what to do with your hair? Asymmetrical styles, out. Too many stylists, say five, with two or fewer customers, not—

"Listen, kid, if you pass by once more without coming in for a haircut, I think it's harassment," said the man with the perfect black, straight-back comb job. His hair came down kind of long on the sides, hanging softly on either side of his face, but the middle bit on top stayed miraculously still, holding the whole show together. He had a sort of pirate mustache and beard, and altogether looked far cooler than I ever figured a hairstylist was supposed to. He stood in the doorway, under a sign that read "Mysterious Ways Hair."

"Oh," I said. "Sorry."

"No, you're not sorry. That hair is sorry. Get yourself in here right now."

"Yes sir."

"Now," he said when he had me in one of the two available chairs, "you have done the right thing. Now it is up to me." There was a third chair, where someone was sitting under one of those Martian helmet dryers, with some kind of towels swirled all around her face. There were no other stylists around. "What is your name?"

"Elvin."

"Good. I like it. I am Nardo. Pleased to make your acquaintance, Elvin."

We shook hands. He had a good firm grip, but mostly from his first two fingers and thumb. From all that scissors work, probably.

"How old are you, Elvin?" He was looking me over now, walking around, crouching low, then boosting up on his toes to get angles on my head.

"Almost fifteen."

"Almost? Almost fifteen. Does that mean that you are fourteen?"

"Yes," I said, my chin dropping guiltily to the navy polyester cloak I now had wrapped around me.

"Well, you look fifteen, I must say. Carol," Nardo said, poking the other body with a comb, "doesn't Elvin look quite mature for fourteen?"

Carol grunted.

"So who did this to you? You can tell me," Nardo said as he began taking exploratory snips of my hair.

"My uncle," I said grimly.

He stopped clipping. "Oh. Well, I usually don't get an answer, since it's actually just a joke question. But okay. Is this uncle of yours the devil, or just a very, very bad hairstylist?"

"He's . . ."

What was he? I didn't know what he was. And what was it about getting your hair cut that made you feel obligated to answer questions?

"I don't know what he is, actually."

"Close family, huh?"

"Well, no, I guess not."

"What do we have in mind today, Elvin? Something radical? Bold? I'm guessing you are looking for something new, because that's why the winds brought you here. Do you have something in mind? Or see something you like on the walls?"

The walls had dozens of pictures, divided equally among men's and women's styles, with very little difference between them. They could have all been the same mannequin with the wigs switched for each new picture. And the truth was, not one of them looked remotely as slick as the maestro himself.

"Can you make me look like you?" was what came flying out of my mouth. I felt myself turn red with embarrassment, but was glad it came out anyway as long as the result was going to be that I was as devilish cool as this guy.

"No."

I deflated. Not in any good way, though.

"You can't?"

"I can, of course. But I won't. Nobody gets to look like me. That's the rule." He pointed dramatically toward the back of the shop, to a sign posted on a door, that read "We are sorry, but nobody can look like Nardo."

"Anyway, my friend Elvin, you are a very handsome young man in your own right. You do not need to look like me. We just need to find the details to complement what you already have."

I reached into my back pocket and pulled out the picture. Of Frankie. It was his most recent class picture. He gave it to me for my birthday.

"Can you make me look like this, then?"

He took the picture from me, stared at it, and expressed himself.

"Oooh, mama. Isn't he nice. Do you know this boy? I mean, he's no Nardo, of course, but he is awfully nice anyway."

I slumped. "That means no, then."

He couldn't quite bring himself to stop studying the Greek god in his hand, but he could spare me a thought at the same time. "Hey, hey, didn't we already have trouble with this? No more of this low self-esteem nonsense, or I will make you ugly. I can do that, too, you know."

"Sorry. We wouldn't want that."

"No. Now about this. You don't have curly hair, for starters."

I tugged at a corner of the picture. He wouldn't give it up. I craned. "It's not curly, exactly, though. It's wavy, really."

"Yes, true. And it isn't as . . . dark as yours, or . . .

48

quite the same texture. And his hair is thick. . . ."

"I have seen the picture, Nardo. Many, many times. Seen the real thing a lot too. I understand the gargantuan nature of the request. I just thought maybe if you were really talented . . ."

"Hmm. An awfully big challenge to set a person for a slow Sunday. But I do like a challenge. You have come to the right place, Elvin. Probably the *only* place."

"Great," I said, clapping my hands, buzzy with excitement now.

"First we'll need to wash this mop." He pulled me out of the chair, led me to another chair, and leaned me back all the way over till my head was in the sink. "So this uncle who did this to you. . . ," he said as he began running warm water and his fingers through my hair.

"Oh, I guess he's probably all right. I'm still getting used to him. I thought he was dead, but he's not. He's out with my mother right now."

"Your uncle goes out with your mother? What does your father think of that?"

"Not much. He's dead."

"Are you sure? You were wrong about the other guy."

"Pretty sure."

"Oh," he said, working some honey-smelling shampoo through my hair with an extra-gentle motion, "I'm sorry."

"It's okay. They're not really out-out; they're at church."

"Oh," he said again, stopping even the shampooing to sympathize. "I am sorry. They always have the worst hair of all."

He went back to his very fine work of shampooing, rinsing, conditioning, and rinsing my hair. It was a pretty relaxing treatment for a haircut, a whole different world from old Sal. I was nearly asleep by the time Nardo revealed that his mother went around telling people that she had had affairs with Jimi Hendrix and Ernest Hemingway and at least two Beatles, but she wasn't certain which ones.

"They will screw you up, your relatives, if you pay too much attention to them."

"I'll try not to."

"Good. And take better care of your hair."

"Right. Less attention to relatives, more attention to hair."

"Bingo. Key to life."

Finally I had the key.

4

Hairy-Handed Gents

Ding-dong-ding-dong.

Mikie's doorbell did not actually make that sound. It was more like the sound of castanets because the little hammer inside the bell got muffled by dust bunnies and his mother liked all things Spanish so she left the castanet sound.

Ding-dong-ding-dong.

But the *ding-dong* sound was in my head as I stood there pressing the button, and had been since I left Mysterious Ways Hair with Nardo waving and shedding tears of joy over my new look, if not his shame in creating it. *Ding-dong* would not leave my head *ding-dong*.

Finally the door opened.

"Oh my goodness," yelped Mikie's mother, Brenda. She rushed out to the stoop and gave me a big hug. Brenda was just shorter than me now, and a lot smaller in bulk, so my being consoled and mothered by her as if I had shown up bloodied and battered was all the more humbling.

51

"Mikie," she called as she dragged me in out of the public's gaze.

Mikie came hopping down the stairs, stopped on the last one, then echoed his mother's concern. Echoed it with a laugh, however.

"Elvin, you got a *perm*?"

"I did not get a perm," I snapped.

"You got a perm, Elvin," Brenda said.

"I did not get a perm! Nardo said he was not giving me a perm. I asked him if I was getting a perm, and he assured me that I was not getting a perm, and I believe him. We are friends. His mother dated Jimi Hemingway, and when I asked him if I was getting a perm, he swore to me that I was not getting a perm, so I did not get a perm, he did not give me a perm, and I do not have a perm."

"Oh Elvin," Brenda said, very, very, very sympathetically.

"Stop that," I said.

"If it's not a perm, Elvin, then what is it?"

"It's a *wave!*" I said, rushing past them both, down the hall, to the bathroom. "A wave, anybody can see this is a wave, a wave."

They followed me down the hall and huddled together in the doorway.

"Oh Elvin," Brenda said again. It was like being

stabbed in the stomach with a hockey stick when she did that. Only she seemed to be in as much pain over it as I was. "I did that when I was pregnant. My God, how I cried. . . ."

"I am not crying; I am not pregnant; I am big boned. I am splashing water on my face because I am hot, not for any other reason."

"Didn't they have any mirrors there, El?"

It is one of the few truly reliable things in life that the word *up* can have two or more syllables when you need it to. "Shut uh-uh-uhp."

I splashed lots of cold water on my face, but it only continued getting hotter. We could make tea off my face now. Mikie's mother went away toward the kitchen. Perhaps for tea bags. I continued splashing, and took a good hard look at myself in the mirror.

I stopped splashing my face and began madly scooping handfuls of water onto my head, then stroking my hair, flattening it down, matting it down.

And watching it sproing back up again. More water, more water. I increased the pressure, slapping myself pretty hard now—and a more deserving head slap was never administered—in a desperate attempt to get the hair back flat to the head where God intended it to be. But the more I slapped, the more the hair worked against me. The weight of the water kept it down for roughly a second before all those curls—waves!—literally bounced back.

"Wow," Mike marveled, "you're actually making it worse."

God, he was right. It was getting taller, tighter, *stronger*. If I flattened it any more, it would be an Afro.

"Brenda," I called desperately.

She came running back to the bathroom. "Yes, hon," she said in *that* voice that made me feel sorry for the poor chump she was talking to.

"Can we . . . wash this out, please? Can you help me here? With . . . this?"

I thought she might cry. "Elvin. Do you know what perm is short for?"

"It is not a perm."

"Whatever it is, it is permanent. You can't wash it out; you have to grow it out. We might possibly be able to do something about the dye job, though, if that's any—"

"It is not dyed. Highlighted. It is just highlighted, to bring out my natural color. . . ."

"To bring out Frankie's natural color," Mike said.

I turned on him like a badger. "Who said anything about Frankie?" I demanded. "What are you pulling Frankie into this for? Frankie's not even here. He's not, is he? What could any of this have to do with Frankie? Frankie doesn't even *know* Nardo, right, which makes

54

you look pretty foolish right about now, Mike."

"Sorry, El, jeez. It was just that you looked a little bit like him for a minute there. Or at least your hair did."

Helloooo?

I turned away from Mikie and toward the bathroom mirror once more. Had it worked? Was Mikie toying with me?

Could I really, in any way, resemble Frank? Was Nardo a genius after all? I looked myself straight in the hair, to give myself an honest summary.

Maybe. The hair was still wet from the struggle and not quite right because Frankie doesn't do the wet look, but maybe. Turn this way just a bit, no, too much, back the other way a little, then, maybe. Squint. Head down. "Turn that light off for a second, would you, Mike?"

"What are you doing? You look like you're practicing to stare somebody down, or pick somebody up."

"Good. Dangerous, yet alluring."

"If you say so, El." He clicked off the light.

There. There it was. Frankie. Or, anyway, Frankie's slightly shorter, heavier, darker, blurry brother.

But close enough. I clapped once and rubbed my hands together.

Which brought up the light like a clap-on automatic light.

And clap-off, no more Frankie. I looked like myself. Except with hair that Barbie would have been proud of in the 1960s. Oh, and fatter. The hair made me look fatter. I slumped.

"Jeez, Elvin," Mike said. He could take no more, came right over and pulled me physically away from the mirror and out of the bathroom with a tight arm around my shoulders. He led me straight into the kitchen and sat me at the table. Brenda put the tea on. I like tea. I like Brenda.

"Stop staring at my mother, El, and talk to me. What is wrong with you?"

"I don't want an uncle."

"What, so you did this"—he gestured at my head— "to scare him away?"

"I'm serious, Mike."

"Maybe you should be less serious."

Brenda brought tea. I thanked her seven times, until she left the room.

"It is serious," I told Mike, "and you know it."

"Right, so okay, it is a shock to have him show up after all this time. Make the best of it. It might turn out great."

"He wants to tell me things."

"Good. You should be told things."

"Maybe I don't want to be told things."

"Oh, there's no maybe about it, Elvin; you do not want

to be told things. That doesn't mean you shouldn't hear them anyway."

"You don't seem to understand. I don't *want* to."

"Consider the possibility that he may have good things to tell you. Like, maybe your insanity is a specific family variety, and he's nuts too and brought the cure with him."

"There is no cure."

"You're hopeless, you know."

"That's what I just *said*, isn't it?"

"Give the guy a chance, El."

"No. He has suspicious hair, he is too skinny, and he took my mother away from me on a Sunday to go to church, and that is not how our Sundays are supposed to go."

"Hmmm."

"What, hmmm?"

"Maybe that's what you're afraid of. That he's going to steal your mother away because he reminds her of your father."

"Oh," I said, standing up so quickly that my chair skidded across the room and bumped into the refrigerator. "Oh, that's just stupid. One, why would I care, if some guy wants to spend a little time with my mother? And two, no way is some stranger going to come along and steal her away from *me*. No chance."

I was losing track myself, of whether I was doing myself any good here or not, but I was getting concerned. The pressure of events, of the last couple of days, was mounting. The dead uncle, the hair, church, it was all gathering in my head and gumming up the works badly.

"The point is, you are worried that Alex is going to shake things up."

"I don't like things shaken." My voice was approaching normal now.

"I know. But I think you'll be making a mistake if you don't give your uncle a chance. Maybe you'll enjoy getting to know him. Maybe you'll learn more about your history and stuff."

"Lucky me," I said. "People chase all over the world trying to trace their roots. I have roots that come tracing me."

"You're magnetic," Mike said with a big smile as his dog ambled into the room. Mike had the only local copy of Grog's scary little reproductions. She looked like a hairy tropical fish or something, but she had a surprising charm that made her seem cuter. And smarter. Possibly because he named her Maryann, rather than, say, Grog. He scooped her up and the two of them grinned at me.

"Thanks," I said. "But honestly, Mike, if Alex has tough stuff to say to me, I don't think I am going to be able to take it."

"Let's test you out then," he said. He stopped grinning. Maryann did not. "Elvin Bishop," Mike said with such convincing gravity that I started sweating instantly, "I am sorry I have to tell you this, but as your hair is drying, it's looking more and more like a Nerf ball."

Well. Well then.

"Well then."

"Just trying to help, El."

"Thank you, Michael."

"Oh no."

Brenda came scurrying into the room. "Did he call you Michael?"

"I'm afraid he did."

I didn't often call Mikie by his full first name. Apparently this had some meaning.

"Calm down, Elvin," she said.

"I am very calm," I said as I shook Mike's hand.

"Right, sure," he said, pulling his hand away from me. "Except that you are never calm. So when you do this, when you pretend to be calm, when you call me *Michael* and shake people's hands and stuff . . . you're not fooling anybody, Elvin."

I patted my Nerf ball head. "Please don't worry. I'll be fine. I probably just need a nap."

"Yes," Brenda said, putting an arm around me and giving a good hard squeeze. "I think maybe if you just go home and lie down for a while, I think you'll feel better when you get up."

I nodded, and headed for the door. Then I thought of something and walked back to Mike and leaned way down close to him.

"How come your dog is so much better than mine?" I said.

I didn't wait for an answer. Whatever my point was, I had probably made it.

The fresh air was good, but really there is only so much fresh air can do. I was actually getting more wound up and not less as I approached my house. What was I going to say to Alex? More to the point, what was I going to listen to? God stuff? Was he here to save my soul? If he was, then could I just surrender it, leave it right there on the floor, and walk away quietly so he could take it and be gone?

The quickest and easiest way to have him gone was what I was interested in, and though I knew that was unfair, I couldn't change my mind.

And that was the state of my mind as I swept through the front door, confident that me and my hair could hurry things along.

Except there was nobody there. And as far as I could tell, neither my mother nor Alex had been there since I left, since they went to church several hours earlier.

They certainly should have been home by then. This was inexcusable, and it had to be all his fault.

Mikie was right. Alex was a dangerous threat to my way of life, intent on turning everything upside down.

He did say that. He did.

And now Alex had even spoiled the relaxing nap I was supposed to have for myself. The downward spiral was dizzying.

Right. The first order of business was to get my hair sorted out. I couldn't be bossing people around the house and telling somebody to get lost and stamping my authority over everything with everyone marveling at my new head. Brenda said it couldn't be washed out, but that was because she had had a perm, the poor thing, and I had a wave.

I marched that wave directly to the bathroom, dropped to my knees at the tub, and threw the taps on full force.

Once my head was soaked, I groped around for shampoo. I grabbed this bottle of bright green stuff with a pump top, and I pumped and pumped away until my head felt like a great big, frothy trifle pudding.

But it didn't smell like that. It smelled kind of appley, and herby. It smelled lovely, in fact. As I worked it through, I started to get some of that relaxation I was hoping to achieve with my nap. I was doing a bang-up job of it too. I would even go so far as to say that my massaging shampooing technique was the equal of Nardo's. And the scent of my hair product beat his by a country mile.

By the time I rinsed the shampoo away, watched as I washed that Nardo, and that Frankie, and that Alex, too, right out of my hair and down the drain, I felt like a new man. I also felt like I couldn't stop humming that song, "I'm gonna wash that man right out of my hair," because once you think of it, it's in there like a tick. I stood and dried my head vigorously with a towel. Then I picked up the bottle of green shampoo and brought it right up to my nose and breathed deeply.

Honestly, it made me feel so good, so cool and collected.

I read the bottle of my new favorite grooming secret.

"For a shiny and flea-free coat."

This kind of bothered me at first. I started barking out loud at the bottle in my hand. "Dog shampoo! Flea shampoo! I was already shiny and flea free. Everything else was a mess, but I was definitely shiny, and I was definitely flea free."

"Aloe Vera and Apple Mint Flea-Repelling Aromatherapy for Dogs."

"What is apple mint? There is no such thing as an

apple mint. Aromatherapy? Dogs don't need aroma-therapy because *everything* is aromatherapy as far as a dog is concerned."

There was an urgent banging on the bathroom door and an urgency to my mother's voice behind it. "Elvin? What's going on? Are you all right? Who is in there with you?"

What do you say?

"I am fine. There is nobody in here. I am talking to the aromatherapy dog shampoo. You forgot to *tell* me that you bought aloe vera and apple mint aromatherapy dog shampoo, and so we are just in here getting to know each other now."

There began some muttering on the other side of the door as my mother tried to explain my erratic behavior to my uncle.

As they talked, I finished towel drying my head, then checked the mirror.

Why do I check mirrors? Why do I subject myself?

Something not unlike a dog whimper came out of me as I took in the results of my long, busy day of careful attention to my hair.

"Are you shampooing Grog, Elvin? Please tell me you are shampooing Grog."

She was hoping against any possibility of hope. No matter how creative she got with the aromas, if I had

Grog in the bathroom, and if she had come in contact with even a drop of water, the whole house would smell as if the toilet was backing up.

"No, Mother. I will show you what I've been doing."

I reached for the door, but not before pausing and taking one last good, long, fortifying sniff of aloe vera and apple mint.

"Hi," I said as I slung open the door.

It was really kind of a treat, the little squeal of horror that came out of my mother at the sight of me.

I pressed my advantage. "You see what happens when you leave me alone on a Sunday?"

"Jee-yeez," Alex said. "What happened to you?"

"This is what the dog shampoo did to me," I said. "And if I were you, I wouldn't get sniffy about anybody else's hair."

"Well," he snickered back, "up until now I'd have agreed with you."

I decided to focus instead on my mother's face. It was frozen, a squinched-up mask of crisscross lines peeking through her fingers.

"Elvin Bishop," she muffled through her hands, "no dog shampoo did that to you."

"Ah-ah," I said. "Flea-repelling aromatherapy."

"I am afraid it is going to repel a lot more than fleas."

She slowly allowed her hands to slide down her face to reveal . . . a mighty effort to keep from laughing. She was biting so hard on her lip it looked like it might burst.

"Hey," I said.

She stopped fighting. "Elvin, sweetheart," she spluttered, and rushed me with open arms.

I ducked, and squirmed past her into the hallway.

"Come here," she said, pursuing me.

Alex wisely got out of the way, flattening himself to the wall before I did it for him.

When she finally caught up to me, I was a quarter of the way up the stairs and she brought me down like a wildebeest.

But once she had me, she was a little kinder. She grabbed me, hugged and held on to me in a way that not only surprised me, it made me feel suddenly very, very important, and warmed. And worried.

"Why do you have to do these things to yourself, ya big nut," she said.

"Well, duh," I said, talking over my shoulder at her because she still had me tackled and pinned from behind. "I think the *big nut* bit should be your first clue."

It was getting just a bit difficult to breathe. My arms were pinned to my sides, the edge of one step was creasing my chest, and another dangerously close to my groin. I wasn't in a great rush to get up, however.

"Why did you get permed?" she said close into my ear.

"It's not a perm; it's a wave."

"Why did you get waved?"

"Because I was afraid my hair was going to look like Alex's hair because of genetics, genetics that *you* have been deviously and quite sensibly hiding from me for all these years, and I wanted to head it off at the pass."

"That's not what Alex's hair looks like naturally."

"Why would somebody do that to themselves on purpose?"

"You did yours on purpose."

"No, I didn't, actually."

"Whew," she said. "That's good. And neither did Alex."

Just then the phone rang. From the other room Alex offered to get it, but Ma said no. She kissed me on the back of the head, then got up. "It's like kissing a Nerf ball," she said.

Next thing I knew, Alex was there. I had flopped myself over and was sort of sitting, sort of lying on the stairs.

"How's it going?" he said cautiously.

"Fine. Where'd you take my mother all this time?"

"We went to church, as you know. Then we went out for some lunch. Then for a walk at the water."

I could hear my mother's phone call going on in the background, weaving in and out of our conversation and making concentration a bit iffy.

Ya, Brenda, he was here when we got here. I know . . . horrendous . . .

"Out for some lunch, huh? And for a walk by the water? Water is nice. I like water."

No, no, he's fine. As fine as he gets, anyway. You know . . . he doesn't tend to cope well. . . .

"We tried to call you, to invite you, but you weren't here."

I know he does. What can you do about it, though? Oh God, I remember, you cried and cried. . . .

"Elvin, I want to spend some time with you," Alex said, interrupting himself, and myself and my mother and Brenda. Compound rudeness.

"Why would you want to do that?" I said because, really, I wondered why he would want to do that.

"Because," he said, but he hesitated too long and I wasn't about to give him the chance to make up something on the spot.

"Because maybe what you actually want is to spend time with my mother. Because maybe that is why you came here at all. I don't have anything to offer you. Maybe you just need to get through me in order to get to my mother and spend time with her."

"Elvin?" Ma said as she came back into the room. Her tone was both indignant and sympathetic. She was one of the great multitaskers, my ma. "Are you grilling Alex, just because we were gone for a while today?"

"You were gone for much more than a little while, I'll have you know."

"You know, it is all right for me to actually go out and do something every once in a while, Elvin. Believe it or not, I do have a life, you know. Or I used to, anyway."

"Don't say that. You did not. You didn't have a life; you had me."

It was getting more serious, my habit of saying things that did not in any way help my cause. I did manage to raise a good hearty laugh out of my uncle, however, which then began my mother laughing, which blended into a comfortable sound that made me uncomfortable, so I joined in just to spoil things.

The three of us were there laughing, and I think Ma believed it to be a big, sweet family moment for us because she came right up to me and squeezed me hard and warm, then went over to Alex and squeezed him not so hard but every bit as warm.

What was going on here, with them? This was giving me the shivers.

"Anyway," Ma said, "you'll be getting your turn tomorrow. Alex wants to take you out for the day."

"What?" I asked with too much vigor. "What? Anyway, I can't. I have school tomorrow, remember?"

"Not tomorrow. I don't want you to go to school. I want you to go with Alex."

Oh my word.

She couldn't want me to skip school. How could she want that? No mother wants that, not even my mother.

"Mother," I said dramatically, "you know I cannot skip school tomorrow. I have band tomorrow. You know full well that the band cannot go on without me. So thank you but no thank you; my music is my life. Good night and good-bye and have a safe drive home."

"Band?" Alex said, enthused. "Band? You're in a band? I knew it. You have music in your blood, you know. I was in a band, me and your dad, when we were around twenty, twenty-one, called the Hairy-Handed Gents. We were great. We warmed up once at an outdoor summer concert before a Harlem Globetrotters exhibition. And now you . . . I just knew it . . . your dad would be . . ."

"He plays the tuba, Alex," Ma said, as if she were straightening him out.

He was undeterred. "Tuba, cool, that's great. I was a bass player, you know, so we're kind of in that same area there, you and me, giving the music some body."

Nothing is more embarrassing than taking praise that

is way off the mark. Like fish that comes to your table with a whiff of ammonia, you have to send it back or it will come to haunt you later. Trust me on that.

"The body they wanted me to bring to the music was the one that fit snugly inside the brass anaconda that is the tuba. I have the traditional tuba body, rather than any aptitude for it. I *oom* about six times per song, and I *pah* about five. Sometimes if I'm bored I don't even blow, I just grunt into the mouthpiece and it sounds pretty much the same. And I can't even count how many times I have been told that I make virtually the same music every day after lunch without a tuba in sight, and so I should sell the horn and just march along with the band a capella, so to speak."

This prompted my mother to swoop toward me with her great mother wingspan extended majestically to come and comfort me whether I liked it or not. Only Alex got to me first.

He stepped right up to me, stood for a few seconds staring at me with smiling, sad, glassy eyes. Then he put both his hands—which were rather hairy, in fact—on my shoulders and squeezed very hard. Very hard.

"Ouch," I said, but very politely since even I could recognize that this was supposed to be a positive thing. I said it like I was just checking. "Ouch?"

"You are a fine guy, Elvin, and I'm sure a fine musician.

The Hairy-Handed Gents would have been proud as proud to have you. Proud as proud."

Me and my tuba sounds had silenced a few rooms before. Even brought a few to tears. But the feeling I was getting now, and what I was almost seeing, was beyond that. Ma looked like she was simultaneously having a tooth pulled and watching me accept a Grammy Award. Alex was suddenly choked out of speech altogether.

"No school tomorrow," she said softly.

"Okay," I said, as much out of fear as anything.

5

Unmonday

I woke myself up. I could not remember that ever happening on a school Monday before. When I came down to breakfast, my mother was already gone. That alone was enough of a shock to my system to have me jittering.

I found my uncle at the kitchen table. He was sitting in front of a plate that held a virtual army of pills and capsules, and half a grapefruit.

He looked up from his feast. "Hi," he said, and gestured for me to take my place in front of another plate, which held toast, grapes, orange and grapefruit wedges, and what appeared to be a bowl of plain yogurt.

"Hi," I said, and stared at his plate.

"They are vitamins," he said. "Vitamins and mineral supplements and herbal stuff and antidepressants, antihistamines and anticoagulants that all combine to keep me ticking. As for your meal, sorry I didn't whip you up one of my truly legendary pepper and sausage frittatas or my cinnamon nutmeg maple French toast, or my banana lemon fritters, or my—"

"Stop it," I said as clearly as I could through the rapids of free-flowing saliva.

"Sorry," Alex said, bearing down on his plate and his big glass of water again. "I'm not quite all there yet until I finish my plate in the morning. I hope you'll bear with me."

"I guess," I said, looking away from his plate toward mine. I thought I might like to trade. "As long as you bear with me. I don't usually have fruit much before lunchtime. Or at least until I've had something dead or inorganic first."

He gulped a small fistful of candy-colored capsules. He gulped a big chug of water. "Right. That can't happen today, though. It's part of what we're at. See, if you had your regular breakfast, you'd probably honk."

Oh, that didn't sound good. That could not lead anywhere good. Because anything on the agenda that might clash with my breakfast . . . would frankly clash with me.

The best course of action, as in all cases of nasty things we don't want to confront, was to duck.

I developed a sudden passion for fruit. I started scoffing orange pieces.

"We are going to the gym first, Elvin," Alex said, then immediately consumed more tablets.

I slowly looked up. I did not stop chewing, but it was an effort. The effort became too much, and I stopped chewing.

"Oh, don't look at me with that cow face. This is going to be a great experience for you. For both of us. It is a really great gym. Has an excellent Olympic-length pool, which most of them don't have, every machine and gizmo imaginable, steam, sauna, whirlpool, the works."

This is how completely and instantaneously I was fleeing from this idea. Before I could even run, my mind beat my body to the back door and began banging, banging to get the hell out.

Alex stared at me quizzically. "Aren't you going to answer that?"

Even he could hear it.

"Your mother's right, you sure are dramatic," he said before going and opening the door to let my mind out like the cowardly dog it was.

Or possibly to let Frankie and Mikie in.

"There, see," Mikie said, pointing at me. Everybody but me was animated as I remained stationary, waiting for everything to pass me by and leave me alone.

"What is that on your head?" Frankie spluttered.

"Hey gents," Alex said.

"Hey Alex," said Mike.

"What did you do, Elvin?" said Frank.

"He got a perm," said Mike.

"It is not a perm, it's . . . Leave me alone."

"Why did you do that?" asked Frank, creeping up closer to me, but very cautiously, as if he could catch this. His tone was of deep concern and bewilderment, as if I had been caught punching myself in the face.

"He wanted to not look like me," said Alex as he scooped himself a spoonful of grapefruit and a pill.

"That is not true," I said.

Mike helped. "No, he did it because he wanted to look like you, Franko."

Frank stopped advancing on me and turned on Mikie. "What? What are you talking about?"

"Ya, he did that to look like you."

"To look like *me*?" It came out kind of like a roar. "Do I look like that? Is that what I look like?"

I must have been trying to sound as weak and unconvincing as possible. "I was not."

"Good," Frank said. "Because I don't look like that. Do I look like that, ever?"

Mikie started laughing at, probably, everyone's expense. "Take a break, will you, Frank? You should be honored that Elvin would risk screwing himself up so badly just trying to be you."

"I was not."

"Elvin." Frank was sounding concerned again. "After

all the work we have put in, trying to make you presentable, trying to pull you up to standard . . . I mean, okay, we hadn't really gotten anywhere but we were trying really hard, and then you go and—"

Alex had cleaned his plate and was now apparently up and running enough to hear what my friends were saying about me.

"Do they always talk this way with you right there in the same room?"

"All the time," I said.

"Well," he said seriously, "that just won't do." He sipped water. "It's no wonder he's a bit of a mess, you guys," was how he scolded them for talking negatively about me while I was in the room. "What do you say when he isn't there, is what I'd like to know."

"I hadn't thought about that, Uncle Alex. I guess now I will."

I dipped pieces of fruit into yogurt, just to be spiteful, but discovered it was not half bad. My day improved, probably as much as it was going to.

"Listen," Frankie said, "I'm sorry. Didn't mean to be cruel about your head and everything, but . . . jeez, look at that head. What are we going to do about it?"

"I like my head," I said. Possibly just to drive him nuts, possibly to work up a little fake dignity, but not possibly because I liked my head.

"You do not," he said. "But we are going to be late. Hurry and get ready, and we'll talk about a plan on the way to school."

Well, at least there was that.

"I am not going to school," I said, and felt pretty chipper about being able to say it.

"What? Why, where are you going?"

Then I remembered where I was going.

Did you ever think that life was just one great big giant evil seesaw that at *best* was never going to let you get away with one nice lovely *up* without immediately jerking you back *down,* and that at *worst* had an enormous, hairy, toothless, rotten kid on the other end who never had a birthday or a bike and who miraculously weighed three times as much as you and took turns first keeping you suspended in terror up in the air while he picked his nose, *then* used his awesome thigh muscles to shoot up in the air and bring you smashing down to the ground so your teeth crunched, and then followed up with the rapid, murderous *up-down-up-down-up-down-up-down* pumping action as he pounded the seesaw between the ground and your groin over and over while you tried desperately, humiliatingly to hang on to what felt like a live concrete pommel horse ramming you up between the legs to the sound of gorgon laughter at the opposing end of the evil seesaw? Did you ever think that? Well, it is.

"Elvin?" Mikie tried after what may have been an extended pause on my part. "If you are not going to school, where are you going?"

"I am going to the gym," I said, my voice exhausted already.

"Why?" he asked. "Are they making you because you did that to your hair?"

"You know, that's a very good question. I don't know. Alex, why am I going to the gym?"

Alex got very businesslike with me. "Because, like I said to you before, Elvin Bishop, I am here to help you."

"Right," I said. "I appreciate that, but can't you help me at the movies, or at a Chinese restaurant or something?"

"That is precisely the kind of help you do not need." He poked me in the stomach, in case I had missed his meaning.

"Cut that out," I said, slapping his hand away. "I thought you were here for *redemption*?" I said it in a broad sarcastic, teenagery way that made redemption sound stupid and therefore would make him feel stupid, which would serve him right for poking my belly and feeding me fruit.

"The two are intertwined," he said with a sort of gentle respect that wasted my effort.

"Listen," Frankie said, "we have to go. Have a fine

time at the gym, guys. And Elvin, we'll do something about your hair after you get that bod all buffed up. If it isn't grown out by then. And whatever you do, don't tell anybody you did this to look like me. That couldn't do either one of us any good."

"Thanks. Your concern is touching."

He nodded and clapped me on the shoulder. Frank's inability to take offense was a phenomenon. It had to be his towering self-esteem that allowed the good ship Franko to navigate the choppiest waters so smoothly. Bastard.

Frank headed for the door. Mikie headed for me. "Pace yourself," he said. "At the gym today, take it easy. You could get hurt, or worse, if you go at it the wrong way and you haven't been . . . y'know, taking care of yourself."

"Hurt, or *worse*? You mean dead, right? There is nothing between hurt and dead. You are hurt, either a little or a lot, and then, when you are worse than hurt, you're dead. You never hear somebody saying that a guy is *worse than hurt*. Oh, how is the victim, is he hurt? Oh no, he's worse than hurt. Are you saying, Mike, that you believe I am such a mess that I might *die* by going to this gym today?"

"Yo, Mike, we're gonna be late. Come on."

Mike checked his watch. "I don't have time, so yes, El,

I think it's a possibility you might die. Please be careful."

"Fine. Get out of here."

Once the door had shut and we were alone again, Alex finished his drink, wiped his mouth neatly with his napkin, then pointed in the general direction of my friends.

"I like them," he said. "Though they could show you a little more respect."

I picked at my fruit, dabbed at the yogurt. "Ya, I guess they're okay."

"It's a nice thing you have going with them. You should value that."

"I will value it," I said.

"It's quite sweet, the way that Mikie one fusses over you, looks out for you. I suspect you probably need a lot of that."

"Your suspicion is totally unfounded."

"And it is plain to see why you are so obsessed over that Frankie one. You're right, he's stunning."

"I am *not* obsessed with anyone, and he is *not* stunning, well, he is, but I didn't say that, and really, I don't know where you're getting this stuff. . . ."

"Calm down, Elvin . . . hey, I bet people have to tell you that a lot, don't they? To calm down?"

"They do not. Nobody ever tells me that, in fact, so you are wrong again. Don't go into the fortune-telling business,

Alex, because you're, like, wrong all over the place."

Once I had put old Uncle A firmly in his place, I grabbed up my mug and took a triumphant sip. It burned me. It was cool, temperature wise, but it burned.

"What is this?" I demanded.

He smiled. "Chai tea plus. I made it a little extra spicy. Stick with the spicy foods, Elvin; that's a good tip. With the hot stuff you can't eat as fast, you can't eat as much, and you sweat. Sweat is a great thing, Elvin."

"You don't have to tell me about sweat. I know sweat better than anybody. Want to see? I can sweat on command. I'll sweat for you right this minute if you like."

"Ah, you should probably save it. Anyway, what I was saying before . . . I wasn't criticizing you. I think it's lovely what you've got. Don't be self-conscious, Elvin, and don't hold yourself back. Live like you want to live. But if I were to give you any advice, I'd say you stand a better chance with the gay one than with the pretty one. You gonna finish that?" He reached across and casually lifted some foodstuffs or other from my plate. It did not matter; as I sat there slack-jawed, he could have stolen all the food and my clothes and the chair out from under me, and I'd have had trouble reacting.

He saw. "Relax, will you, Elvin?"

I spoke very relaxed. Almost dead, even. "What gay one?"

"Mikie."

"Mikie is not gay."

"He's not? Hmm. Okay."

Well, that was easy enough. I felt better already, having addressed the issue and stated my—

"What do you *mean* I would stand a better chance with the gay one than the pretty one?"

"I just mean, I think that Frankie is a kind of tall order. That he's probably got so many—"

"No, no, no, not Frankie, we all know about Frankie, this is not about Frankie, why are we always talking about Frankie . . . I mean, what kind of *chance* am I supposed to be after with anybody?"

I may have finally been scaring him. He stared at me in a kind of wonder, which may have been fear.

"You seem to have a little crush, that's all."

"A what?"

"A crush."

I let it sink in so I could discuss it in a more rational and mature way.

"A what?"

"A crush."

I whipped down my chai tea just as quickly as I could. Then I thumped my cup on the table loudly. I fixed my uncle with a steely stare, as if I had settled something. Then I called my dog.

The only time Grog responded to her name was when I called her from the kitchen table. I couldn't be just in the kitchen, or even *near* the table, but had to be seated, with some kind of food action plainly visible in front of me. She wouldn't even get excited like a normal dog if I was standing by the front door with her leash in my hand because she felt exactly the same as her master about physical activity, which meant I had to throw sticks and stones *at* her in the park in order to exercise her.

But she came right to me when I called, and I almost even detected a wag of one of her back parts as I produced the tea bag.

I looked at my uncle, then at my dog.

Munch. Gulp.

She loves used tea bags. I found this out when I caught her tearing through the garbage, climbing over perfectly delectable chicken bones and moldy cheese to devour our many soggy tea bags.

And from the look of it, chai was her new favorite.

"There," I said smugly, "would a gay guy's dog do that?"

Alex grinned from ear to ear and shook his head. "Elvin Bishop, my nephew, whatever it is you are, I am glad you are it."

"Good," I said. "I am not gay. Mikie is not gay. Nobody is gay. Now I'd rather talk about something else."

"Fine," he said, clapping his hands, "go get your gym gear."

Gear? My gym *gear*? *My* gym gear? Even that sounded painful.

The power of suggestion. You know how when you become aware of something you don't think you should do and so you become overwhelmed with the urge to do it, like pressing a button that says *emergency* or laughing when you're in trouble, or eating a stick of butter? Well, I had one of those now. I could not stop thinking about Frankie. And about . . . the other issue.

"Mikie is not gay," I said to Alex as we stood in front of the wide and clean glass-front entrance to the Bantamweight Sport and Racket Club.

"Right, you told me."

We stepped through the automatic doors and were immediately greeted by two receptionists with excellent teeth and fat-free arms that looked like braided rope off tall ships' rigging.

"Hello, Alex, good morning, Alex," they said brightly.

"They know you? Just like that?"

"I'm a member," he said. "So are you."

"How is that? I have never even been to a gym. I have never even walked along the same side of the street as a gym."

"I got you a membership. But you have to be sixteen, so you are sixteen. And I got one for your mom. You're paid up for a year."

"Who's your friend, Alex?" the lead receptionist asked.

He said, with shocking but obvious pride, "This is my nephew, Elvin. My late brother's boy. Lester's boy. Elvin Bishop."

"Well, I'm pleased to meet you, Elvin Bishop," she said, and held out her hand. I took it, and she squeezed me too hard. That was okay, though. It was very okay. "Will you be a guest with us today, Elvin?"

"Oh no, he's a member in his own right," Alex said. "He just needs to get his picture taken for his ID."

"Super," she said, and led me over to a microcamera mounted on her desk, like a sinister surveillance thing that always distorted your appearance far worse than you ever could have distorted it yourself.

God, no. My distortions. Now not only was I going to be photographed with the fish-eye lens that would make me look like a snowman in a fun house mirror, but there was also the other, stupider distortion.

I reached up and felt my head, to check for the thousandth time if it was all a horrible dream.

It was, unfortunately, a horrible reality. The Nerf fluff and texture were still there. I wondered how heavy my head was going to get when I jumped in the pool and absorbed half the water.

I stood in front of the camera because I was told to. It clicked, not waiting, not caring whether I had primped enough to look presentable, and within microseconds I was holding in my hand a card declaring my membership in the Bantamweight Sport and Racket Club. Or so I would have to assume, since no way was I looking at it.

I followed my uncle past the reception desk to the turnstiles, where you had to swipe your card to get in. We went in side by side and swiped together.

A little *bleep* sounded when the bar code was read off the cards. Followed by, yes, our member photos, flashing high on the television monitors mounted above the turnstiles.

"Oh crap," I said, scurrying past the monitors and shielding my eyes from the burning rays of my image. "Why do they do that, so they can do, like, before-and-after pictures if you get in shape, or don't-let-this-happen-to-you pictures if you don't?"

"They do it so staff can see that the person using the card is the actual member." Alex steered me down a corridor toward the locker rooms. "Everybody's picture is bad, Elvin, so it's nothing to get worked up about."

"Not as bad as mine. I bet they're talking about it right now at the desk. I bet they're making copies of my picture right now and turning it into their screen savers."

He pushed open the door to the changing rooms.

"It's important in life to appreciate that the whole world doesn't exactly revolve around you, Mr. Bishop."

"You know, I wish it didn't. But until I receive reliable evidence to the contrary, I'm going to continue believing that it does."

My uncle laughed, then half backslapped, half shoved me into the room.

It was mostly filled with old guys. Not bashful old guys either. Naked, or nearly naked, all over the place. Getting into or out of tiny bathing suits on their way to changing out of or into tiny underwear, it was bikini geezer town everywhere I looked.

One shiny-head guy sat on a bench in front of a mirror blow-drying a vast field of snowy chest hair. When I walked past he looked up, nodded, and winked at me. Another one had his feet pulled up onto the bench and was blow-drying the spaces between his toes—as well as the scrotal area between the spaces between the toes. I averted my eyes from him, which of course was averting *toward* this other one, so I finally just put my hand right over my eyes.

Which was when Franko popped back into my head. He even had chest hair now, auburn and curly like all the rest of his hair—

Stop that, Elvin. Stop that right now.

I stared at my feet, as staring at my feet always calms me, and I finally made it to the locker next to my uncle's.

"I wish you wouldn't say that," I said, "about Mikie being gay."

"Well, firstly, I'm not anymore, you are. And secondly, what does it matter?"

"It doesn't," I said, because no other possible answer sounded any good. "Anyway, you can't tell just from looking at a guy anyway, right?"

Alex stared at me then, which made me squirm.

"What?" I said. "What? Do you see something? I can explain—"

He grinned, shook his head, and said, "Item number four fifty-two on the Elvin Project: acquaint subject with the broader spectrum of humanity."

"Hmm," I said, "I'm kind of having enough trouble managing the spectrum I know."

My phone bleeped just then. The screen said it was Ma. "See," I said to Alex, shaking my head solemnly at the burdens I faced.

There were many phenomena that went into making my communication with my mother the precious tribe-of-two closed system it was. One of the least helpful, however, was that whenever we talked on our mobile phones to each other, we sounded like we were on string-connected tin cans and there were fifteen of us on the party line. Very shy people at the heart of it, we Bishops, and to be out there, in the world, right in front of people, felt sordid, dangerous, and vaguely embarrassing, causing us to speak quickly and repetitiously and in alien tinny voices.

That was my story, anyway. She, actually, couldn't get enough of it. I think she would actually work it out on a little map somewhere, the point at which I'd be at my most awkward.

"Ma."

"Elvin."

"Ma."

"Elvin."

"Ma. Ma, what are you doing, Ma? I'm with, like, the guys here. Everybody's naked, and I'm embarrassed enough."

"Really? Don't be embarrassed. Don't let any of them snap you with towels. I know how those locker rooms can be. And if they make fun of your mole—"

"Ma! Nobody's interested in my mole."

"Did you wear your good underwear?"

I had to go cool. "Mother, *all* my underwear is good."

"Hmm," she said, in that tone.

"Fine, don't believe me. You didn't call to talk about my underwear and my mole, though. What is it?"

"Hmm," she said, but differently. "I just wanted to check in on you. Just wanted to make sure things were all right, with you and Alex and all."

Just then Alex started tapping me on the shoulder to get moving.

"Ma says hi," I said. "Listen, Ma, I have to go."

"Okay," she said, oddly tentative.

"Is everything all right?" I asked.

"Of course," she said. "God, you are such a worrier, Elvin."

"I know," I said. "So why don't you just leave that to me."

"Call me later," she said.

"I'm a very busy man," I said. "I'll try and fit you in." I hung up.

"Do we belong to a seniors gym?" I asked Alex when three more muscular history professors walked in.

"No," he said. "It's just that time of day. There are a lot of retired guys now, after the pre-work rush hour and before the power lunchers. It's my favorite time, actually."

I found myself staring very slyly around the room while changing.

"Do they come every day?" I asked.

"Don't know. Probably most. Why?"

"They're all in better shape than me."

"Well there you go, the benefits of regular exercise well into the autumn years."

"No, I mean, like way better shape than me. Like, probably every one of them could beat me up. Scarylike."

There really were a lot of muscles in the room. Some very rounded bellies, some elasticated bums that didn't come all the way up off the bench until the owner was already standing, but really, a good deal more tone than I had come to expect off these kind of—

"Alex," I said, alarmed, grabbing his arm. "That guy there blow-drying his armpits, he keeps winking at me."

"That's okay. They do that. It means, hello, how's it going."

"Well, he's asked me how's it going twice already."

"Maybe you should stop staring at everybody while they're dressing then."

I was indignant. "I was not . . ." I had turned, finally, to face Alex, only to find him ready, in long, brown sweatpants and charcoal T-shirt, while I stood with my street clothes still on, albeit around my neck and my ankles. I shut up and faced my locker and got the job done.

"It's okay to peek, though," Alex said as we entered the gym proper.

"I was not peeking," I whispered angrily.

"'Course you were peeking. Everybody peeks. How else are you going to know?"

"Know what?"

He led me to a mirror wall. "Do what I do," he said, and spread his feet very, very, unwisely wide. Then he reached for the floor.

"Do I have to—"

"Yes."

I did what I could, within reason. I watched the two of us in the mirror, with the background of healthy people of various sizes and ages bouncing and pumping merrily along on machines behind us. Alex had his hands close to the floor, head down, fingertips almost touching the carpet. I looked very much like a bullfrog, knees bent like the big cheater that I was, almost squatting, arms resting on my thighs.

Alex held his stretch long enough, then straightened up. When I tried to do the same, he clamped his hands on me and started arranging me like a store window dummy. He kicked my feet sideways, farther, farther out until they were crying from missing each other. They had never been separated before. Then he pushed my upper body forward and down. "You can do it," he said.

I did not want to lead him on. "No, I can't."

"I can get you there."

"No, you can't."

This went on for a few more minutes until I began making sounds like those realistic crying baby dolls when you flip them over on their backs.

Finally he let me up, but it was only so that we could perform much the same duet through standard toe-touchies ("Everything God wants me to touch is already within arm's reach, Alex,"), calf extensions ("Ankles are only supposed to bend the *other* way; I saw it in a book,"), and the thoroughly perverse thigh-stretch thing where you bend over forward while pulling your foot up in the air behind you so you look like one of those self-feeding bird doohickies on people's desks ("Did my mother say you could do this to me?").

Through it all I was made to watch the poor, fat sap in the mirror, and I wanted to cry for him, then I saw the relief on his face when it was done, and I wanted to cry for him. I didn't cry, though, because it wouldn't have been a very gymly thing to do, and I was afraid one of the old tough guys would come over and slap me like General Patton.

"Wow," I said, wiggling around to feel every screaming, betrayed muscle I had. "That was tough. But I'm glad I did it. Thanks, Alex."

This close. I was this close to crying, no matter who I embarrassed, when he told me that that was just the warming-up part.

Fortunately we were on the bikes, and I was sweating like the rain forest within seconds, so my red face and teariness wouldn't bother anybody.

"So what did you mean," I said, "everybody peeks because how else are you going to know?"

"Everybody wants to know," he said insufficiently. You would think he was the one needing to conserve breath.

"Know what?"

"Know what everybody else has got, and in what proportion."

I wouldn't have imagined my face could get any redder than it already was. Which just showed the limits of my imagination. Why did they *have* to have mirrors facing you from every vantage point? Were they not aware that some of us were here for the very reason that looking at ourselves was a very painful experience? On top of the painful experience of torturing ourselves with these evil contraptions. There had to be some skinny guy behind that mirror, with all his skinny friends, with nice wavy hair, watching us and laughing and eating whatever canapés they wanted to without worrying about it at all.

Red face aside, I had to ask. "Are you saying guys are all . . . looking at each other all the time? Looking at, like, all their stuff?"

"Yup."

"Like, their stomachs, and their muscles, and . . ."

"Yup. And especially the type of guys who come to a

place like this. Comparison is rampant. Though not as obvious as what you were doing."

Not sure here what I was thinking or what I was hoping to get out of it, but right at that point I began pedaling madly on the stationary bike very much like a person who thought he could escape any and all unpleasantry pursuing him.

What I accomplished, of course, was exhaustion and nausea.

"It's okay, Elvin," Alex said nicely. "It's natural."

He stopped pedaling and got off his bike, which caused me great joy because that meant I could too.

"Really?" I said.

"Really," he said.

That was a relief. He put an arm around my shoulders and led me across the room.

"And don't worry about your anatomical incorrectness. You'll be fine."

When I stopped short and froze in the middle of the room like a statue, Alex did not. He continued right on and plunked himself down in the seat of some weight-lifting machine.

My anatomical incorrectness.

I was not to worry about it.

You know, funny thing was, I hadn't considered worrying about it recently.

"What are you doing?" Alex called across the way, squirting the fire with lighter fluid. "Come over here, will you?"

It was like I was released. Like there was a giant elastic band previously attached to my waist that had now been cut. I ran—toddled like a giant baby, really—toward my uncle.

"What incorrectness?" I demanded quietly.

"Oh, Elvin, it's not anything—"

"I don't want to talk about it," I snapped.

"Good," he said. "Now here, sit at this machine next to me. It's just got about thirty-five pounds on it, so you'll be fine. Just push gradually, away from your chest like I am here, and—"

"Is it my mole? It's my mole, right? I'm never coming back here again. I can't believe I took my mole out in public."

"Lift the weights, Elvin; you'll feel better."

I lifted the weights.

And here's the miracle: I felt better.

I pressed the weight off my chest, extended my arms all the way, held it a couple seconds, then let it down again. I was mimicking my uncle's motions, and it was working out fine. Push up, breathe out, drop it back, and breathe in. I did this twelve times and stopped when he told me to.

My arms felt. My chest felt. Felt not like I had pushed over a building, but like, anyway, something was inside them at least. I could feel blood moving through my upper body, where it was usually just pooling there.

And my head. My head was just a bystander in all of this. But my head felt like it loved it.

I did another set. Felt even better. We moved to other machines, ones to isolate my biceps, my triceps, my pectorals, and give them the attention they deserved. Muscles that had been isolated in a completely different way up till then, isolated right out of any thought I ever had. I could feel my muscles getting gradually, no, rapidly, weaker and wibbly as time ran out on my weightlifting experience. But it was a good kind of wibbly, even when I was killing myself on the most unnatural machine that made me push my arms together, trying unsuccessfully to get my elbows acquainted with each other, but very successfully to bunch up a lot of fleshy material in front of me.

But I noticed a more unexpected thing going on. Alex was wearing down even quicker than I was. He was, in fact, just sitting on the seats of the machines through most of my last few stops. Occasionally he would put up a lift, or put one halfway up. Then he would adjust the weight down again, try again, and stop again. By the end he was just keeping me company.

"Are you all right?" I asked.

"Sure, ya," he said through short, shallow breaths. "It's just that the weight bit, it's really not my thing. I just do it, really, as a part of the program. Keep my weight up, keep me stronger."

"Keep your *weight* up? I never heard of that. Is that a thing that people do?"

He laughed a wheezy laugh, then stood up.

"Ya, some people. And it just makes me feel a little unwell from time to time. I'm better with the other stuff. Let's take a nice walk together. You want to take a nice walk together?"

"Sounds good to me," I said, and followed him to the treadmills.

And he wasn't kidding. I hadn't paid too close attention before, but it was obvious now as I checked out my uncle's back view. He did not share my physique. He was a very lean model Bishop indeed. And when he walked, his knees never quite straightened up all the way. He didn't look built for weight lifting. Or for walking, for that matter.

But walk we did. We sidled up on adjoining machines and headed off for the horizon yonder. Or, our reflections in the mirror yonder.

"Elvin," Alex said over the hum of the treadmill and the padding of footfalls. Then, when he was supposed to say something more, nothing happened.

I looked at his reflection, waiting. His reflection looked back at me. There was no sign that anything more was coming. There was a friendly smile, at least.

"Was that a question?" I asked after a minute. I clocked it on my red digital display panel. I had also burned fourteen calories.

"Nah," he said. And then, nothing.

I clocked another minute. My face started flushing again, my sweat building up again.

"Did you want to ask me any questions?" Alex said. "I figure, after all . . . there must be questions."

I thought about it for nine seconds. "No, thanks."

"Ah, come on."

"Okay. Right, how old are you?"

"That's your question?"

"Ya."

"Okay. I'm not yet fifty."

"What a coincidence. I'm not yet fifty myself."

"There ya go. Loads in common."

"Really? What else then?"

"Your dad."

Sweat was coming thicker now. On both of us. We were not setting such a torrid pace, just a brisk stroll really, but it was enough.

"And?"

"Food. We both love food."

"Maybe."

"Maybe? What does that mean, maybe? You telling me you're not sure you love food?"

"No, I'm saying maybe you don't. I never saw such a skinny food lover as you before. I think maybe you're an imposter."

"Hah," he laughed, then coughed a little, then slowed down his treadmill a tic. "I wasn't always like this. I was nearly as big as yourself once upon a time."

"You were not."

"I was so."

"Wow. How'd you fix it?"

"You wanna know?"

"I wanna know."

"You really wanna know?"

"I really want to know."

"Ah, you don't really want to know."

I was thinking about coming over to his treadmill and tackling him to demonstrate my desire to know. Instead, I reached over and yanked the little emergency stop cord on his machine and stopped him in his tracks.

That was when I could hear him panting and wheezing.

"Thanks," he said, mopping his brow with a sweat-gray wristband.

I kept walking, and staring at him. My intense footsteps

sounded thumping loud and intimidating now. Must have been what broke him.

"Okay," he said, his breathing more even, "the trick is, you gotta curb your appetite."

Then he slapped me on the back and started walking toward the door. "I can't do this anymore, Elvin. I want to head down to the pool area. You staying here, or you want to come down?"

Curb your appetite? The answer to mankind's biggest, fattest, sweatiest conundrum is to *curb your appetite*? No way, this matter was not closed.

In fact, so anxious was I to catch up with Alex and yank from him the secret of the waist smaller than the inseam, that I forgot to shut the treadmill off. I instead sort of pivoted—no, pirouetted—on the moving mat, found myself startled and disoriented with the floor moving beneath me, then *surfed* for the last 1.2 seconds before being dumped, on hands and knees, on the rug.

I looked around quickly for the most important thing, to see if anyone was watching, and only almost all of them were. I returned to the machine, coolly and politely wiped away my sweat, then tailed after my uncle.

"I can't curb my dog, never mind myself. How can *curb* be the whole answer?" I said when I caught up to him at the lockers. He was sitting on the bench untying his sneakers.

"Because," he said, pausing to look me in the face. "Because it just is. This is the story, nephew. This is a lot of what brings me here. Appetites. The only real answer, to everything, is getting your own appetites under your own control. I'm gonna be straight with you here, Elvin, so stop me if at any point you can't deal with the reality of—"

"Stop," I said.

He looked startled. He looked disappointed.

"It was just a joke, Alex. I do want you to talk."

"Oh. Good. Thing is, appetites are the devil."

"Stop."

"It wasn't a hilarious joke the first time, Elvin."

"No joke now. Question. I just wanted to know before you went further, if this is going to be a devil and Jesus and all that kind of talk, because if so maybe . . . maybe not."

"No, it's not. Not really, anyway. I meant the other kind of devil. Just, what bedevils you. Your own devils. Yours, mine, like that. Nephew, appetites are our curse. Your dad, he got killed by appetites. Your dad ate and drank and smoked himself to death. My appetites have been trying to get the better of me for forty years. Bishops been appetiting themselves into oblivion for as far back as anybody cares to look, and if anybody cares to look at you, young man, they would have to conclude that you are an A-one example of a Bishop. And I care to look."

I could probably count on my thumbs how many times in my life somebody had talked me into submission. If I wanted to keep track anymore, I was going to have to sprout a third thumb.

For several long seconds my uncle stared up at me, waiting to see what I was going to do about all this.

But I wasn't going to do anything but stare back. I was choked up and choked back about some part of what my uncle had to say, or all of it, or what there was yet to be said that hadn't been said, but I didn't know which, and it didn't matter. It wasn't even that he brought any fresh bolts of lightning, because if I was in a completely honest mood, I would say I recognized that message like it was the phone number of an old friend I never called anymore.

Alex knew as much, or his face was good enough to say so, and then he went silently back to undressing and redressing for the pool.

I was looking forward to going to the pool, which sounded like relief, though it would probably turn out not to be. I dressed as quickly as I could and tried to keep my attention focused on my own business, even if peeking at somebody else was truly the done thing. I did not have to do it.

Except that I did.

I let my eyes wander as Alex stripped down. I didn't think about it; I just did it. I didn't want anything out of it; I just did it. I didn't control it or feel good about it; I just did it.

And I did it modestly, but that was enough. For when I let my eyes fall on my uncle's feet as a starting point, I saw something. Or, the lack of something.

He had two toes on his right foot. And they weren't even consecutive toes. They were the first and last toes, the dad and the baby toes, with what seemed like miles of pink, crinkled skin in between them. There was even a pattern to that skin, like the pinchings along the crusty edge of a homemade pie.

"The trick to the peeking is not to get so hypnotized that you forget that you are not, in fact, invisible to others."

"I was not peeking." I had kicked my sweaty sweats away and was desperately shoving myself into my bathing suit in that hurried way that causes the inside liner to get all rolled up and then one leg hole shrinks to about one-tenth your actual leg diameter so you get the one leg in and wrestle flamboyantly with yourself and your suit and your leg, hop-spinning in an awkward semicircular, seminude version of a dance you might see at an old-world wedding.

"Do you want some help with that?" Alex said with a laugh.

"No, I do not want help with this," I said, finally surrendering to humiliation—I should really carry a white flag with me at all times—and unrolling the now completely balled-up bathing suit down over my legs before easing it smoothly back up again.

"Less hurry, more speed, as they say," he said.

"Is that what they say?" I said.

"I think so. Now what do you say we head for the pool."

He headed for the pool, showing me his back.

This time, it had to be on purpose, what he was showing me. No peeking was necessary.

Alex's back, his narrow, pale back, was pocked with a small minefield of what looked like bullet holes trying to heal. But if they really were that many bullet holes, my uncle Alex was the Terminator. Or the undead.

Either way, he was shaping up to be a pretty unhealthy-looking guy for somebody with a health club membership.

I followed him, and as we walked through the big foot trough where you are forced to delouse your feet before going into the good water, I could not help myself. Under the six inches of water, the foot took on 1950s horror creature features, like a big, pink, elongated crab of a foot, and there I was staring again.

"A bunch of your toes are not there, Alex."

He looked down, shocked. "Damn. They must have come off in my sock again."

I hopped, briskly, out of the foot wash pool.

He followed me, briskly.

"Diabetes," he said, catching me by the arm and holding on.

"What?"

"Diabetes, Elvin. Diabetes ate my toes."

"You have diabetes?"

"Sort of. I did have it, just like lots of folks in our line, I'm afraid. Gotta watch yourself there, young Elvin. You got sweet blood. We all got sweet blood, which is our flavor.

"But I had the diabetes and then I didn't. It got fixed. Doctors put me on a diet and some pills. They cut out all my favorite sweeties and replaced them with all manner of sugar substitutes. Got cancer from the sugar substitutes, though, so I guess you'd have to call that a win-some-lose-some, good-news-bad-news, Lord-giveth-Lord-taketh-away result there."

"Cancer? You got cancer and diabetes?"

"Not anymore. Cancer went away. I got better. While I was in prison."

I stopped walking and firmly removed my arm from

Alex's grip. I faced him down. Well, I didn't face him down. I frankly didn't even know what facing somebody down would look like, unless it was like when Grog had an accident on the floor, and then when I saw it I stared at her and then she faced down at the rug rather than facing up at me. And even that example wouldn't entirely hold up because *accident* was an inaccurate word because Grog soiled the carpet intentionally and even came out to the kitchen and tugged me gently by the hand to show it to me, just like Lassie bringing the sheriff to the fire down at the old mill. She's so like Lassie, Grog.

So I didn't stare Alex down because I did not know what that was, but I did know that if you did it you probably did not do it to a graduate of the United States penitentiary system, if in fact Alex had ever been in jail.

"Were you in jail, Alex?" I asked in a low voice.

"I was."

I sighed. "Why does everything have to happen to *me*?"

Once again I had made my uncle laugh, which I did not understand but which was fine with me. I left him, took a running dash to the pool, boldly right past the No Running sign, and I dived in.

I felt different—which almost always means better—the instant I broke the surface of the water. Being under there, cool and wet and airless, weightless and soundless, was joy.

You probably caught me there lying. You probably already told yourself that *joy* was too strong a word. Okay, but only just barely.

For one thing, I stayed under that water for a good long time. No, wise guy, not like a rock at the bottom, but like an actual swimmer type. I stroked and stroked with about the same motion as a seal or a penguin, but funny as that may seem, the comparison felt right and flattering to me. Because those were creatures that looked comical and misfitted on land, but once underwater they were perfect. They were, in fact, flying.

I was, in fact, flying. It had been so long since I had dived into a pool, I couldn't even remember. It had been so long that my bathing suit, which was purposely bought seven sizes too big, was now only three sizes too big. I had forgotten I liked to swim. I had forgotten I could swim.

"You can swim, boy," Alex said to me as I popped up out of the water with a great intake of air. He had caught right up to me even though I had swum the whole length of the pool without coming up. "I knew it. I knew you would be a good swimmer. We are fish, you know. Bishops are fish. I think we slithered up out of the primordial soup a little more recently than most of humanity, because every Bishop takes to water just as readily as to air. Good, Elvin, this is good to see. I'm happy to see."

He sure was. You would think he taught me himself, the way he was grinning and carrying on.

And it made me want to dunk right back under the water so I couldn't see him or hear him celebrating my ability to swim.

So you know what I did? I dunked back under the water, of course.

The silence was heavenly, the feel of the water was heavenly as I felt it slide over me, as I made my sealy way through the pool with my slick underwater stroke. Stroke. Stroke.

When I broke the surface once more, something amazing had happened. I had swum underwater the full length of the pool again.

I wasn't even winded.

Of course I was.

I was so winded and grunting that the pool attendant gave me a long, worried look, but that wasn't important because I swam underwater the whole length of the pool without coming up for air. Even when I saw my uncle splashing the place up with his overexcited, understylish Australian crawl as he hurried to get to me, I didn't feel the need to get away again.

I didn't feel the ability to get away again either. But really I didn't feel the need.

"You are a swimming sonofagun," he said when he got there, panting twice as hard as me.

Never ever thought I would be able to assemble those words in that order: *panting twice as hard as me.*

"Stop," I said, taking charge because my breath was back, and because I was feeling in charge all of a sudden.

"Stop . . . what?" he panted.

"Everything. Stop everything. I don't want to hear how great it is that I can swim. You know what I want to hear about? Missing toes and jail and . . . did you say antidepressants? . . . and antidepressants and cancer and *you . . .*"—I poked him hard in his scabby chest, raising an immediate angry red welt—"and *sorry* about that . . . and bullet hole scabs . . . and my mother . . . and what's wrong with my penis . . . and my father . . . and . . . I can't think of anything else right now, but I am sure I will . . . I'm afraid I will . . . and if I don't, I bet you will come up with something new that I won't want to know about but then I'm going to need to hear about because you couldn't leave me alone so you had to come along and spoil everything . . . and so you better explain yourself. . . ."

By the time I had finished, if I was even finished, Alex's breathing had completely calmed. Calmed, in fact, to the point where I could not detect any rise and fall of his chest. It had come to the point where I was noticing such things. I got suddenly extremely nervous. Was he breathing? Was he okay? Had I damaged him further?

I dived back under the water.

But this time he caught me. Two firm bony hands gripped my shoulders before I could slip away and pulled me up.

"Let's go to the sauna," he said, holding me tight so I couldn't escape. "They have a nice sauna here, a wet sauna. So many places now, they won't let you ladle the water onto the rocks, and the dry stuff is hardly worth your time. This one, you'll like. It's a nice place to talk, too. Best place for talking. And it'll help clear up that skin of yours some too, when we open up those pores. . . ."

"There is nothing wrong with my skin," I said, but went along. "My mother says my skin glows."

It certainly glowed once we stepped into the sauna. It nearly caught fire.

"It's hot in here," I said, stopping just inside the glass door. It was a six-foot-by-six-foot cubicle of mostly cedar, with three tiers of benches rising at the back. Alex climbed to the top and took a seat.

"Yes, it is hot," he said. "It's supposed to be hot. That's what a sauna does."

I reluctantly took a couple of steps in. "Well, why does it do that?"

"It's good for you. Makes you sweat."

"A ringing telephone makes me sweat. The new fall TV schedule makes me sweat."

"This is different. You'll see. This is the kind of heat that does stuff for you. Makes you tough."

"I've only been in here for a minute, but I get the distinct feeling that I am getting tender, rather than tough."

He sighed. He closed his eyes and leaned back, letting the heat attack him.

I took a seat on the bottom bench. The truth was, this wasn't so bad, so far.

"Why do you sit up there?" I asked.

"Hot air rises. The heat's better up here."

"Okay," I said, feeling confident. I rose to the second level.

Not bad. The heat was a little drier than I had expected, actually making me less sweaty than when I walked in. Face feeling a bit flushed, a bit tight. But the overall effect was kind of tingly. This was all right. And it was not difficult. I liked things that were not difficult, and if this was something that was both not difficult and good for me— well, that was kind of my Holy Grail right there.

I ascended to the top level, taking my seat a few inches away from my uncle. Who may have been sleeping by then.

His arm reached out and slapped me on the knee.

"Glad you could make it," he said, without opening his eyes.

"Ouch," I said, my knee skin turning out to be a bit heat sensitive.

Alex opened his eyes. He looked at me, then over to a wooden bucket that sat near his feet. "You mind if I ladle on some water?" he asked.

Why should I mind? Water was always one of my favorite things. Water, especially in the heat, was always a welcome thing. "Why should I mind?" I said. "Can I do it?"

He nodded, handed me the ladle, and pointed me to the metal electric barbecue thing with the hot, dry stones on top. "Just make sure the water gets on the rocks, rather than on the grill or the wall or the floor. Cover those rocks, boy."

Boy, I covered those rocks.

Then I sat back in my top-row seat. It was very interesting, the way the steam crawled up the glass of the door, making its way to the top, then to the ceiling, then along that ceiling toward us.

The first whiff of the steam was a rush.

It was the last thing I could call a rush for a while, because almost instantly that steam became more like a wave of boiling molasses descending over my body, coating me in lethargy.

"I think I'll get down now," I said slo-mo.

"No, Elvin, don't," Alex said, holding me in place quite unnecessarily. "This is the stuff. This is what you come here for. This is the best thing for us. Let the heat engulf you. Let the sweat pour. Let your mind drift, your spirit float. . . ."

He continued talking. He continued talking nonsense. He went on and on about the spiritual, physical, mental properties of this sauna business, and *mental* was right. He claimed all kinds of amazing things were going to come of this, but the only one that seemed to be coming true was sweat. Gallons and oceans of sweat. He compared this uncomfortable and unenlightening experience to a Navaho sweat lodge where people would go in and not come out until they had hallucinated and collapsed and all but croaked and they began jabbering like monkeys about all the important things in life.

"You're nuts, Alex," I said, and I must have meant it since it took about all the strength I had to say it.

"I might be," he said calmly. "Anything else you want to tell me?"

"No," I said.

"Okay," he said.

"You're gross," I said.

"I've heard that before," he said.

"You don't have enough toes. Those scabs on your

back bother me. You have scary hair. You are too skinny. I don't like having you around," I said.

"That makes me sad," he said.

"We had an okay life, me and my mother. It wasn't great, but it wasn't all complicated, either."

"Debatable."

"Not debatable."

He leaned over and before I could stop him, sloshed another big helping of water on the rocks.

"Oh God," I said as the steam came like a fireball toward my head. I tried to squirm down to a lower level, but he held me by the elastic waist of my bathing suit. Weak and slimy as a snail, I remained stuck to my seat.

"Are you going to kill me?" I asked.

If he was a film madman, he would have laughed. He did not laugh, which scared me more. "Why would I kill you?"

"Well, you were in prison."

"I'm not going to kill you."

"How long were you in prison?"

"Some years."

"How long you been out?"

"Some years."

"Where have you been since you got out?"

"A lot of places. I don't remember all of them, to be honest, from before I quit the drinking and the drugs and stuff. It gets clearer after that. Mostly around here, though, is where I've been lately. Been around here pretty much the last couple of months."

"Here?"

"Here. Keeping an eye on you, checking you out."

"What? No. No, that couldn't be. Watching me?"

Watching me. Just the idea of it, of being watched. Even if I knew I was being watched, even if I was watching someone watching me, I was always self-conscious to the point of hysteria wondering what I was revealing about my inner self through the antics of my outer self. If somebody was watching me over time and I was not aware of it? Oh God.

"I'm sorry," I blurted.

"What?"

"Whatever I did. Whatever it was you saw, I apologize. I'm not usually like that. I wasn't myself that day. It was my first time, and I didn't even like it. A bigger kid made me do it. I was just trying to fit in—"

"Jeez, will you stop that. You have nothing to apologize for."

"Really?"

"There's nothing wrong with you, Elvin. You're a great kid."

"You sure you were following the right guy?"

"Damn. Where'd you get all these hang-ups?"

"Same as everybody, from my mother."

"Your mother is far cooler than you are."

"You leave my mother out of this," I said, standing up quickly and getting a rush of blood to my head. I wasn't going to sit down, though, and spoil the strength of my moment. "You keep your hands off my mother."

I stood there, wavering in the vapor-rich air of the top of the sauna. Alex reached for the water bucket. "And you keep your hands off that ladle, too," I demanded before thumping back down into my seat.

He relented on the ladle, but not on my mother.

"I didn't bring her up," he said, "you did. And as long as you did, let me point out that another thing we have in common is that we both love your mom."

"I never said that," I said. "She is good. She's got her problems. I like her, right? Hey, we're no different from any other mother and son, all right, so why doesn't everybody just stop saying—"

"Wow," Alex said, "could it be true? Could it be, nephew, that you are not able to say you love your own mother?"

I thought about his impertinent question for a minute. Then I thought about it for another minute. Then I fell right over sideways on that top bench, struggling to breathe.

"Shut up," I said.

"Elvin Bishop, that is very sad. That is so very . . ."

His voice trailed off. I turned my head to look up at him. He was coated in running sweat streams like I was—well, not like I was since I was perspiring so much it looked like there was an invisible barbecue chef basting me—so it was hard to read his face. You could read his body, though, all slumped and shrunken. He said sad, and he meant sad.

"You gotta tell people you love 'em," Alex said softly. "You gotta do that, Elvin, you just gotta."

Now he was making me very sad, because, apparently, I had made him very sad. This hardly seemed fair. How did all this bad stuff get in the sauna, when there was none here when we arrived? It was like a nuclear reaction of crappy feeling.

"I am extremely hot, Alex."

"Stop changing the subject. You do that a lot, don't you?"

"Why were you in jail?"

"Because I stole money. Have you ever told anybody in your life you loved them? Once, even?"

"I am very, very hot. Who'd you steal money from?"

"Everybody. Do you ever miss your dad?"

"Why do you take antidepressants?"

"Because I can't take everything else anymore. Do you ever get mad, that he's not around?"

"Maybe I get mad that you *are* around."

"Maybe you do. I don't mind. But I can tell you that I miss him. I miss your dad, and I get mad sometimes that he isn't around, and I loved him and I still love him, and your mom, too, and you too, ya portly bastard, I love you."

You know, I didn't even mind that. *Portly* didn't bother me, hardly even registered, even. As I lay there, my vision getting all wavy as my head went for a molten metal swim, I felt more and more like my fat was indeed burning off me. I felt it melting away. I heard it *pish-pish-pishing* away a drop at a time onto the hot whatever between the slats of our bench. I got through the bad, torturous part of the sauna sweat lodge experience, had paid my dues, and was coming out somewhere else, where you were rewarded for your toughness by great gifts of health and lightness of thought and burning-away blubber.

I barely looked up when somebody opened the door and stepped inside. I barely looked up when he came over and sat on the bench right below Alex and me. He was an older guy. A heavy guy with thin gray hair that had a shiny skullcap of skin on top, and rounded shoulders. He sat down heavily. He breathed heavily.

Then he reached for the water ladle.

Oh God, no. Don't do that. I thought it, but I didn't say it.

He ladled on one big helping of water. Then another. Then another. The sauna filled up instantly with the kind of fog that filled old black-and-white movies with England in them, though England never could have gotten this hot. I could hardly see Alex now. I could hardly see the man. I could just about make out the shiny patch on his head.

He ladled on more water. Then he did it again.

"Could you stop that?" I wheezed into the void.

He stopped, turned halfway around, and halfway smiled at me.

"He's a good kid," Alex said.

There was a thick pause. "He is," the man said. "You're a good kid. Do you know you're a good kid?"

I shrugged. "So I hear. Thank you."

"Good manners," the man added. "You've been brought up well. There's not enough of that. There's never enough of that. Most kids aren't any good, but you're a good one. Mother must be proud. Bet she's proud. She proud?"

"Well . . . we don't really talk about it. . . ."

"Then you should. When you get home, talk about it."

Sounded enough like a command that I said, "Yes sir."

I heard, just then, the quick open-shut of the sauna door.

"Alex?" I called, because I thought it was high time we

left too. I was skinny enough now.

He didn't answer. "Alex?" I tried again. Nothing.

I got right up, slowly. My head still spun, and my knees wobbled. I made my way carefully down the steps and across the slick floor to the door.

"You're a good guy," the man said before I hit the door. "Keep being a good guy. Don't turn into a jerk when you get older."

"Okay," I said.

I jumped out the door and snapped it closed behind me.

"There you are," Alex said. "Why didn't you answer me? I kept calling you."

"Can we go now?" I said.

He smiled weakly and started hobbling toward the locker room, looking half as strong and twice as old as when we had arrived.

I scooted up and bumped up alongside him, sort of propping him up with my shoulder.

Or possibly propping us both up.

6

The Wednesday Trick

"I can't go to school. Alex broke me."

"Elvin, that was two days ago. It was really pushing it to stay home yesterday; today is out of the question. For goodness' sake, you worked out at a gym; you weren't in a train crash."

I knew I was going to school, obviously. I was dressed for school. I had my school stuff with me. I had my note explaining that I was absent the previous day because I had to care for my sick mother—I wrote it, she signed it—and I had my hand on the doorknob. I never minded going to school, and truth was my body didn't hurt all that much anymore. I didn't expect to win the debate, but I was hell-bent on prolonging it.

And I had no idea why.

"Elvin?" Ma asked.

"Yes?"

"You are going to be late. You're not even trying at this point. Stop staring at me, and get to school."

I stared at her a little more.

"What's wrong, pet?"

Maybe twice a year she called me *pet*. Made me want to pull in and retreat from the world. Retreat back into about 1995.

"I don't know, Ma," I said. "I don't feel right. I don't feel like myself. I feel like I don't *know*."

"Like you don't know what?"

"Nothing in particular. Just, like I don't *know*. Usually, even when I don't know, I kind of feel like somehow, I *know*, you know? But right now I don't know, at all. You know?"

She took in a deep breath through her mouth, whistled it back out through her nose.

"It's Alex, yes?"

"It's Alex, yes. But it isn't. It's me. It's me and everything else. Alex is stirring stuff up, that's for sure. But it feels even bigger than that. Like up till now I had a fairly clear notion of myself and how I fit into everything and how everything fit around me. I mean, I wasn't master of any universe by any stretch, but I didn't feel lost. Now? Right now, I don't have any clear notion, any sure view of myself and everything else."

There was a pause. I gripped the doorknob harder. I could at least be master of the doorknob.

"Oh, shut up, Elvin."

That was me, speaking. I suddenly got sickened by me and my running mouth and I wished I could suck it all back in.

"No," Ma said, and grabbed my hand as it twisted the doorknob in a lame attempt at fleeing. "There is nothing wrong with speaking your mind, Elvin. I'm glad you did. I would be terribly worried for you if I thought you were bottling all that up. And . . . now, don't get angry here . . . I have to say, what you just described to me was a pretty fair definition of puberty."

"You *promised* not to use that word," I said, rattling the doorknob like a prisoner.

"Fine," she said, "fine, I won't. I just wanted you to be aware, that there is a lot of stuff probably at work on you now. That this is all terribly hard but perfectly normal, and you aren't going crazy. Other than the fact that adolescence is basically a form of mental illness."

We did some more staring.

"Thanks," I said with a little sneer. "You always know what to say to make me feel better."

"I know," she said.

And you know what? She did. I felt better. Not a lot better. But better.

"Now, I'll need to drive you to school so you're not late."

"Now, you will," I said.

There was more to it than that, of course. I felt, as I was heading back to school, like I was returning from some around-the-world trip, or from some pagan right-of-passage ceremony where they dump you in the jungle for a month to survive naked and without any pre-packaged snacks.

Or like maybe I was unchanged, but the world I was reentering had morphed in my absence.

"Have you heard from Alex?" I asked as we neared the school.

"No," she said.

"Where is he?"

She shrugged. "Wherever it is he stays," she said. "He declined to give me a phone number or anything else. Said he'd be back. He always was fond of the old clandestine."

"Well, he's hardly going to be able to *fix* me with that kind of consistency."

She pulled in front of the school as the last stragglers slipped in through the big metal front doors. She shifted into park.

"Do you want to be fixed?"

I thought about it for a few seconds. "I don't think so."

"Good," she said brightly.

"But I think I do want to listen to him for a while. I

think I want to know more."

"Good," she said brightly. She slapped my knee. She made me smile.

One thing that had not changed in the last few days was God's sense of humor. First period was gym.

All my muscles were contracting in horror as we entered the locker room. But that was not it. The physical pain and exertion of dodgeball and rope climbing, the ritual humiliation of my utter inability to master even one of the several individual skills that contribute to quality basketball, these things paled next to the real problem.

Frankie and Mikie were in my gym class.

As we were getting changed, something we had done in scores of gym classes before without notable incident, I became terribly aware of one of the big somethings that were wrong with me.

I was suddenly awkward with my two best friends.

What was wrong with me? Was I that weak minded, that a couple of random potluck observations from an uncle who didn't know anybody could change my whole view of me and my friends?

Yes.

I was shy, I was embarrassed, I was guilty. Guilty? I was curious. I was rudely curious. As we changed, and as I fought this thought with everything I had, I was just about powerless to refrain from sneaking peeks at both Frank and Mike.

And it wasn't even *that* kind of peek-sneaking, even though it was still in the back of my mind that it was okay, that everyone did it, that I was free.

No. I was looking *into* them, somehow. As if there were actually something there, that I could see, that was going to enlighten me somehow about what existed down deep inside that could tell me an important *more* about them.

Or, about myself.

I was doing it, I was doing it clumsily, and I was aware of it. But I couldn't stop.

"What are you doing?" Mike asked. He was standing at the locker next to me, pulling up his shorts. For his part, he didn't seem particularly bothered one way or the other what I was doing. Just curious. Mike, much like my mother, was expert at never being alarmed at whatever I did.

"Nothing," I said smoothly, bending down to tie my laces.

"Yes, you were, you were staring at me. What, am I getting fat or something? Cut it out, will ya?"

His manner, treating it like it was just another oddity of mine, was reassuring.

"Go back to staring at Franko; he likes it."

Well, that didn't help. Mike pulled on his shirt and headed for the gym. I scurried after him.

"Seriously, Mike," I said, "is that true? Am I always staring at Frank?"

"Uh-huh."

I was so distracted and disturbed I didn't at first even realize the attention I was getting from all the other guys. But one by one practically everyone in the class made a dash my way in order to give a playful bouncing pat to the sponge that was my head. I had almost forgotten.

"I cannot believe how bad this thing looks," Frank said when it was finally his turn for a pat. "You are brave, Elvin, I'll tell you that. If it was me, I'd kill myself."

"You'd kill yourself if you got a zit," Mike said.

"I think that would be the honorable thing to do," Frank said.

I just stared at him. I stared at him hard and consciously. Not, as it may have appeared, out of pathetic admiration. But to gauge myself. To see, now that I was aware, how it *felt* when I stared at Frank. To see how I felt, about how it felt.

I needed answers, and I needed them now.

I was really kind of floating out there for a minute until Mikie squeezing my arm brought me back.

"Do you want to talk about something, El?"

"What?" I asked. "No," I answered.

Mikie shook his head. "I think you do."

I didn't say no this time. I didn't get a chance to say anything before the PE teacher's horrifying scream of a whistle sliced the air and was followed by the more terrifying words, "Okay, all line up for choosing up sides for basketball."

At least I could honestly say the day wasn't going to get any worse after first period. It didn't get noticeably better, either. I could not concentrate on a thing, and helpfully wore my daydreamer/out-to-lunch expression all day so the teachers didn't have to search too hard for a slacker to mock in class. And did my hair make the task that much easier? Well, you could hardly blame them.

"Are you okay?" Mike asked as we hit the street when the school day finally consented to die.

"I'm okay," I said in such an unconvincing dial tone I almost blurted *liar* at myself.

"Is it your hair bothering you?"

"Of course my hair is bothering me. My hair is bothering everybody. But that's not it."

"Ah, so there is an *it*."

Sheesh, he could be exhausting.

We were on our way to our weekly Wednesday afternoon chill-out session. That means bowling. And I needed to bowl like I'd never needed to bowl before.

"Can't we just bowl?" I asked.

"What," he said, "and not talk at all?"

"Ya," I said.

"No," he said.

Franko was suspiciously quiet. He normally had a poorly informed but convincingly delivered opinion on everything. Now he was just sort of drifting along behind Mike and me. Not very alpha Franko at all.

"And what's with you?" Mike asked. Mike woke up on the *I'm the daddy* side of the bed today, which was really not such a bad thing. We even called him Dad on those days. It gave the world a slightly better feeling of rightness. Mike's the guy you would want to do the driving if you suddenly had to take over the space shuttle or the world.

Frank just stared at me.

"Well?" Mike said.

"His hair. His hair is really upsetting me. Your hair is really upsetting me, El."

We decided to let him be quiet for another while.

I felt better when we entered the bowling alley and submerged ourselves in the fluid of bowling alley sounds. The nice baldy guy behind the counter knew us and had our three pairs of shoes up by the time we reached him. He never said anything to us, which was cool.

"What happened to your head?" he said.

Already I didn't have the strength for this conversation anymore. "I fell down," I said.

He felt bad for me. "That's terrible. Lane seven."

In lane seven, as we laced up our shoes, I was reminded of other conversations I didn't want to have.

"So Elvin," Mike said, "what did your uncle do to you?"

"What are you talking about? My uncle didn't do anything to me."

"He must have done something to you. You aren't the same guy since you came back."

"Well, we're always trying to make me not the same guy, so that must be good, right?"

"No. Don't be ridiculous. Franko, you're up."

Franko always bowled first, followed by Mike, then me. We liked things always the same. Same is good. Change is bad. I always won, by the way. I was the best.

If you'll allow me, I would like to repeat that. I was the best.

Bowling was life's only endeavor that provided me the opportunity to say that. This may have been why we bowled every Wednesday and at some point on most weekends. It was my pals' weekly contribution to propping up my floppy self-esteem.

"We don't want to change the basic you, Elvin," Mike continued as Frank bowled. "We just try and help you out here and there, with suggestions, advice. But one trip to the gym with Alex seems to have you shell-shocked."

Frank was bowling poorly, as usual. Because he was watching all the other bowlers more than the pins in front of him, as usual.

"I'm not shell-shocked. But . . . Alex is missing all his toes."

"What?"

"Well, not all of them. But all the middle ones on one foot. He had diabetes. And he had cancer. And he said I better watch out because I have sweet blood and would you call my Franko thing a crush?"

"No," Franko called in the middle of rolling what was very nearly a gutter ball.

Mike stood up for his turn. He smiled me a Dad smile. "Is that what's bothering you?"

"Maybe," I said. "Nothing is bothering me, but maybe."

"So what?" Mike said. "Millions of people have a crush on Franko. In fact, nobody has a bigger crush on Franko than Franko, and look how happy he is."

"It is not a crush," Frank said, shoving Mikie off toward the lane. "It's admiration. And that's fine."

The two of us stared silently at Mike as he went through his Steady Eddie routine of sizing up the pins, feet together, six perfect steps, nice follow-through. After three balls, he had an eight. He always got eights in candlepin. It was hypnotic, reassuring.

"So what if it was a crush?" I said to Frank.

"Are you trying to tell me something?" he said.

"No, I'm trying to ask you something. You can tell by the way my voice goes up at the end there."

"So what if it was?" asked Mike, returning to the table. He was staring at Franko as he said it.

Frank pondered a few seconds. "I think the rules say I'd have to beat him up," he said, without either malice or humor. He sounded as if he were just working out an *If Sally had fifty-five cents and wanted to buy three nectarines at five cents and twelve strawberries at two cents* problem.

"Is anybody else hungry?" I asked.

"Frankie, chips and Cokes," Mike said. "Low man buys, and we already know you're our low man, so you might as well just go buy now."

Frank just shrugged. I figured he was happy enough to exit the conversation.

"It's not a crush," Mike said as I got up to do my bowling.

I lined up my perfect form. I was made for bowling. I had a bowling body.

I said that out loud one time. Once.

I addressed the pins. I gave them names. I sensed their

fear. I intimidated them mentally, I started my approach, my long strides, my backswing.

My bleeping telephone.

I stopped, pulled the phone out of my hip pocket. I was one of those jerks who hears even the tiny mobile phone tone as some kind of authority figure that I must obey.

But it was no authority figure; it was my mother.

Our usual tin can sounds were even more symphonic here in the bowling alley.

"Do you know what I'm doing, Ma?" I grouched.

"Of course I do, you wild thing, it's Wednesday. You are bowling and you have your burgundy socks on."

"I do not—," I started, looked down, stopped.

"I wouldn't bother you, except Alex is here looking for you."

"Alex? Why is he there now? What does he want?"

"He wanted to see you, I guess."

The sound of every ball in the place, especially the sound of every ball rolling down alley six or alley eight next to me, sounded as if it were originating inside the phone.

"Well, he cannot see me. I am bowling. Or, rather, I am standing halfway down alley seven talking on the phone, watching other people bowl."

"I could send him down," she said. "I'm sure he

would love to watch you."

I yelped, loud enough to interrupt quite a few other bowlers. I waved at them, the universal bowler's apology signal. "He cannot come here, Ma."

"Fine. He probably wouldn't like you with your bowling face on anyway. But here, I'll put him on."

"No!" I shouted, and had to do the wave again.

"Is that any way to talk to your ol' uncle?" Alex said.

"Sorry, Alex," I said. "I wasn't shouting at you."

"No, you were shouting about me, though."

I was about to be stupid and deny it. "Sorry," I said.

"Don't worry about it. Hey, you know your dog peed on the floor here."

"Well duh," I said, "it *is* Wednesday."

"Uh, right," he said. "Listen, since you're busy, could I see you tomorrow then?"

I was standing there with my phone in one hand and my ball in the other, looking back up the lane to where Franko was crumpling up his chip bag and starting right in on mine. "Ya," I said. "That'll be okay."

"Great," he said. "Can't wait. By the way, I hear you are a great bowler. So was your dad. Here's your mother."

"Hi," she said.

"I hate it when he says that stuff. About me being like my dad."

"Do you?"

"Well, no."

"I didn't think so. Have a good game, Elvin."

"Okay, I'll try."

I hung up, put away the phone, and addressed the pins all over again. I picked up my stride right where I'd left off.

And threw my first gutter ball since I was about six.

"What's he doing?" I asked when I returned after fighting my way back to a respectable seven on the frame. Frank was hunched over his shiny, slick, silver-plated mobile phone. His thumb was working furiously.

"He's sending a picture of himself," Mike said.

"To whom?"

Mike pointed over to lane two, at a pair of girls. "He went over and got their number while you were up. He promised them a picture."

"My phone can do that," I said, just to get his attention. "But I've never had a chance to use it. My mother already has pictures of me. Will I send one down to lane two? Tell them we're twins?"

Frank jumped up out of his seat and glared at me as he went to the line to bowl.

I sat with Mike.

"That your mom on the phone?"

"Yup. And him."

"Alex?"

"Ya. Grog did the Wednesday trick for him."

"That's our girl. What did Alex want?"

"Wanted to see me. Wanted to come here."

"Did you tell him to come?"

"Are you kidding? I threw a gutter ball after talking to him on the phone. Imagine what would happen if he was here."

"Right. We wouldn't want to risk your average over something like, you know, family."

"Correct."

As if we were starting a new, lane seven salon, Franko was now standing just where I'd been standing, also using his phone instead of bowling. He was more productive, though, since he alternated between shouting down to lane two, and texting them.

"I'm going to see him tomorrow, though," I said.

"Good."

"I guess. I do want to see him. I want to talk to him and hear stuff before . . . while he's here. But I think I'm afraid of him too. I think the same things that are kind of interesting and exciting about him are scary at the same time. Like finding out all this little stuff that I do that makes me like my father was, maybe. I don't want to hear that, do I?"

"Of course you do."

"Of course I do. But why does it bother me so much at the same time? Why does it give me the shivers? Why am I glad to see Alex and at the same time I want him to go away? And does everybody peek in the shower at each other?"

"Everybody?" Mike asked, staring up at the projected scoreboard. "I wouldn't know what everybody does, El. Everybody's different. Don't worry about what everybody is doing. That'll make you nuttier than you already are."

We both looked to Frank now, standing with the phone on his shoulder, the ball in one hand, the other hand on his hip, and a great big smile on his face. He looked like Michaelangelo's David statue in bowling shoes.

"Him?" I asked.

"Probably once upon a time, he stared, to check people out. I don't think he sees the point anymore."

I waited a respectful pause. Too late.

"Sometimes," he said without looking at me.

Another pause. Not too long.

"He scares me, stuff he says. Alex. He's like death. And when he talks about my Bishop bloodline, he sounds like *my* death. And he looks like death. Maybe he really did die, and now he's been sent back to fetch me."

Mikie turned away from Frank, and the scoreboard,

and all the rest of the bowling-related activities, to look me square on. His eyes were close enough to mine that I could feel the little flutter of it when he blinked.

"I don't think you are in any immediate danger, El."

"Do you think I'm gay, then?"

"Did Alex say that?"

"Not exactly. But he made me feel gay. And he has been in prison."

It was like Mikie had become one of those mind-control guys, his beaming eyeballs forcing me to reveal all. Even if I had no idea what *all* was.

"Would you know what it was like, to feel gay?"

"Well. I guess I'd have to guess. Would you know what it was like?"

I didn't know where that came from. That's stupid, since of course I knew where that came from. That came from one of those things Alex put in my head that was bothering me so much. About Mikie being gay. A thing that was none of my business and surely shouldn't have been in the same league with other things like, oh, my death, but somehow was there, right up there with my death. Somehow, the question of was Mikie gay had even passed the question of if *I* was gay, on the big chart of big stupid questions.

"Did Alex say I was gay?" Mike asked calmly as he created a little more space between our eyes.

"Sort of," I said. Then I rushed to add, "But he didn't say it like it was a bad thing. I don't think Alex thinks anything is actually a bad thing."

"Ya," he said, "I could see that. Tell you what, Elvin. I'll answer your question if you answer mine first."

Crap. I hated these. These were never any good. These were always mind games, and while mind games with Franko were pretty safe, with Mikie you could be in some dangerous territory.

But you also couldn't very well say no.

"Go," I said.

"Right. My question to you is, do you *really* need for me to answer your question to me?"

I leaned farther back away from him. I was not composing a response. A warm wash of relief came down over me.

I grinned. "I'm never playing that with you again."

The two of us sat back and watched then as Frankie lifted his shirt and sent an electronic picture of his stomach muscles five lanes away.

7
Shut Up and Wail

School was letting out, but it wasn't letting me out. We reached the end of the corridor where Frank and Mike were to head straight out into the sunny afternoon, and I was turning right down the dark hallway of band practice.

"I wonder what he wants?" I said, and everybody knew who I was talking about because I kept talking about him.

"He just wants to see you," Mike said.

"He saw me already. There's nothing more to see."

"That's not true," Frank said. "The hair keeps changing. Every day it's taller and wider, and another new color. And by new color I don't mean it's changed from what it was. I mean a new color as in a color that never existed anywhere before."

"Don't you have someplace to go?" I said.

"Yes, as a matter of fact, I'm meeting those two girls from the bowling alley. You want to . . . oh, that's right, you have band. Guess I'll take Mikie. Mike, you up for it?"

Frank wasn't looking for an answer. He was already headed for the door. Mike, smiling, turned to me and shrugged his answer. Not that it mattered.

"Not that it matters," Frank said, holding the door. "They're both mine."

They were gone, and I was heading down the hallway, enjoying the small bit of peace between the squonk of classtime and the squonk of band.

Spleep-spleep. My phone. In the near-empty cavernous hallway of the school, the sound was like some evil Hitchcock bird coming to get me.

"Hi, Ma," I said.

"Hi, Elvin, how are you? You sound very echoey. It seems like every time I talk to you on the phone, there's feedback or echo or zoo noises or something. Do you need a new phone so we can have better conversations?"

"Ma, I have to say, the fact that you call me up to talk about my phone, that's the kind of thing that affects the quality of our conversations."

"*Anyway,* I can't stay on long because my boss thinks I'm on the phone to you too much as it is. She says she doesn't believe this is a fourteen-year-old I'm talking to all the time. Says it's got to be either a boyfriend or a six-year-old. I told her you're a little of both."

"Ma!" I said, my mortified voice bouncing around the walls and coming back to mock me two and three times. I looked around and found no one to be embarrassed in front of. I was deeply embarrassed just the same, my cheeks like toasted marshmallows.

"Oh, don't be so stiff, Elvin. Here, why I called. It just occurred to me, why did I see Grog inside your tuba this morning? Don't you have band?"

My tuba.

I took my phone and did what I do when my phone makes me mad. I rubbed it back and forth over my forehead, then my temples, the way truly hypertense people do with the heels of their hands.

The tiny voice came from the side of my head, "I'm guessing from the grinding sound that you did have band today."

"Yes," I said flatly, the phone now in traditional phone position.

"What are you going to do?"

"I have to go. I just have to sit there and read the music and go *oom-pah* with my mouth at my parts. The band teacher says it's to help me keep progressing with the rest of the band when I forget my instrument. I say it's to make me look like a turd when I forget my instrument."

"You won't look like a turd. You'll be cute. Right, I

have to go. Don't forget you have Alex coming this afternoon. So get right home after band."

Thursday used to be one of my top four or five days of the whole week.

It wasn't full band practice anyway, which was a break. It was brass ensemble. The county held a music festival every year with competitions and prizes in every conceivable category of classical caterwauling, and for weeks we were broken up into our specialties to practice.

So today I was in the basement, in Practice Room C, with my brass ensemble—Neil Patterson on flugelhorn, Callum George on trombone, Tobias Kolb on tenor horn . . . and Elvin Bishop on deep, foolish noises.

"Again, Elvin?" Callum sighed when I walked in *sans* tuba.

"Hey, lighten up, will you. I have a lot of stress."

"God," Callum said, "not the hair again. You're not going to blame your hair for this, are you?"

"No, I'm not going to blame—"

"Then it's his mother," Tobias said. "I bet he's going to blame his mother."

In between wisecracks the ensemble punched the air with blurps and honks from their respective brass weapons, so the atmosphere was quite festive.

"You can't blame your mother for everything, Elvin," said Neil. *Bwooorp.* "It's just not cool."

This wasn't the X-Men, it was the brass ensemble here, ranking on me and instructing me on what's cool. If my reputation had reached this woeful state, I had to consider the possibility that I was partly to blame.

"I don't really blame and complain like that, do I, guys?"

They decided to answer through the medium of song.

Bweeerp. Bloop. Fweee-fwee-fwee. Gaarrruup.

"Well then," I said.

"On the bright side," Tobias said, "you are getting pretty good at the tubeless tuba."

"Thanks."

We had normally twenty minutes to sharpen up before Mrs. Llewellyn came to start the hard-core drilling, and we had to make use of that time. She did not tolerate dull or slack playing, and if we weren't already good when she got there she made us play "Mandy" over and over until we broke. So we saddled up our instruments—I saddled up me—and tore right into "The Foggy, Foggy Dew."

Tobias was right. I was getting pretty good at this. I sounded better without my tuba than I did with it, and while this had the potential to become a problem down the line—say when I needed to play the actual tuba in front of actual people—right now it was kind of rocking.

"*Oom,*" I called out. "*Pah,*" I answered. "*Oom-oom,*"

I said, and *"Pah-ahh-ahh."*

I was jamming. The other guys were pretty good too.

"You gotta be kidding," came the loud, brittle call from the doorway. It was Alex. He was standing there with a baffled expression on his face and my tuba around his little hips.

Beepety-beepety. My phone.

"Hi, Ma, how are you?"

She spoke in a rush-hush. "I think Alex is coming there."

"I think you might be right."

"Is he there now?"

"Well, my tuba just came in with something trapped in its coil. I'd better go before it constricts."

"Have fun."

"Do I ever have anything else?"

"Elvin," Alex said, "that was the silliest thing I ever saw, and I have seen some silliness in my time."

I walked over to him and gently removed the tuba.

"If you followed me around more, you'd see plenty of silliness to beat that."

"Sounds like an invitation. I accept."

How do I do it?

I tried the here's-your-hat approach. "Well, thanks for bringing this, Alex. . . ."

"Don't mention it. Your house is far too easy to break

146

into, by the way. I have to speak to your mother."

"You broke into the house?"

"Well, that tuba was hardly going to get itself down here. When I talked to your mother and she told me. . . ."

I knew this had to be traceable to—

God, I do blame my mother for everything.

"Are you going to introduce me to your band?"

"*His* band?" Callum George spluttered.

Cripes. "Callum, Neil, Tobias, this is my uncle Alex."

"Hi, guys," Alex said with real enthusiasm. He then went around and shook hands with each of them. "I was in a band myself when I was younger. Called the Hairy-Handed Gents. You probably didn't hear of us. . . ."

I wished he hadn't left that dangling in the air like that, like somebody was required to respond. I was aware here of one of those special moments I had missed out on with not having a dad: the scorching embarrassment they could produce.

"I think maybe I did," said Tobias Kolb graciously.

"Ya, maybe," said Neil. "It sounds familiar."

I liked my band.

Alex was beaming, even if he couldn't possibly be believing it. "I played with this guy's dad. We were hot. I played bass, so you see we got a musical legacy here to live up to."

"Maybe *legacy* is a little too—"

"Hey," he said, happily interrupting me, "we had a motto in the Hairy-Handed Gents: Shut up and wail."

"Cool," Tobias said. "Can we use that?"

"You can if you shut up and wail," he said.

One of the good things about brass is, if you want to wail, you have to shut up. And so we did both, for my uncle.

We played our "Foggy, Foggy Dew," this time with me on actual brass. It was nice. Better than nice. We blended better than usual, all of us hitting our marks just right, all of us peeking at Alex over our music stands as he gently but clearly did the job of conductor/timekeeper with his bony hands swirling the air between us. A beautiful small, contented smile clung to his face as he concentrated on the notes, and floated on them.

I was all over the place. Not musically, as my *ooom*s and *pah*s were impeccable, but in my head, and in my heart. Alex was embarrassing. He was weird, and he was still scary. He was death on legs, even more so now than he had been a couple days earlier. But at the same time, in this time, in this place, when I could see him on a whole different plate, there was a different something else about him.

He got lost in what we were doing here, and in getting himself lost he gained something else, something nice, and innocent. Which I don't think is any small trick for a veteran of federal incarceration. And he looked like a kid, too. An ancient kid.

I had to admit I was worried just how badly the guys were going to take this. I feared they were going to see Alex as a total freak, as a joke, and if I saw them passing around those unmistakable looks . . . I'd have been mortified, and I would have clocked every one with my tuba. One of the few great things about tuba, it being the best weapon in the orchestra.

But it wasn't necessary. They didn't exchange the looks. They were too preoccupied watching Alex. They were liking it, liking him, liking all this. I guess I had forgotten we were the brass ensemble here. We suffered geeks gladly, and appreciated any appreciation.

And appreciation it was. Alex directed the music, hummed the music, bobbed his head and squinted his eyes like he was drifting off somewhere better than the dull, damp cell we were squonking in. Then he did one better.

"Can I have a go?" he said before he had even stopped his maniac clapping at the conclusion of "The Foggy, Foggy Dew."

"What?" I asked. "A go at what? The tuba?"

He nodded wildly and came at me.

I extricated myself from the tuba with some difficulty, and some trepidation. There was still some essence of

Grog wafting up every time you pressed a valve, so I had some hope he wouldn't have the stomach for this.

When was I going to remember, Alex had the stomach for everything. He'd already experienced everything.

He slipped into the tuba, smiling broadly, looking it all over like he was test-driving a new car, fingering valves, tapping the mouthpiece.

"See," he said to his attentive audience, "since I was a bass player, this contraption is not entirely foreign to me. I know how to lay down the bottom to the music."

He blew into it a few random times, producing some muddy notes. His sound was not entirely amateur, practically as full as mine when I blew, though not quite as nice as when I played the invisible tuba.

"There were four guys in my band too," he said wistfully, seeming to disappear a little into the instrument. He looked like he might have been looking at his reflection in the center coil where the Grog oils would have made the shine brilliant. "So we have that in common as well. And one of them looked just like this"—he pointed to me—"so this is all practically a big fat flashback for me. Though to be truthful, Hairy-Handed Gents–related flashbacks are not unknown."

He looked up from the tuba, out of his reflection, out of himself, into me.

It kind of hurt. It was kind of great, the way he was

looking at me, and it kind of hurt. Looked like he felt the exact same.

"Now, if you'll indulge me, I'd like to play you my signature tune. Actually, it's every bass player's signature tune, 'Smoke on the Water,' by Deep Purple."

All the other musicians in the room looked blankly at one another. The bass man blew.

Blum blum BLUM
Blum blum BLUM-BLUM
Blum blum blum
BLUM-blum.

And that was it. Whatever *it* was. Alex lowered the horn from his lips—or rather, lowered himself from the horn in a kind of serpentine withdrawal that left him crumpled on a stool and wheezing like a train. I ran to him just as the tuba was pulling him to the floor.

"You okay?" I said, pulling it off him.

"Great," he huffed, "great. Did you hear that? I still got it after all this . . . time."

"Ya," I said, and I meant it. He had it, all right. It wasn't music, but *it* he had in abundance.

The other guys were clapping politely and thanking Alex just as Mrs. Llewellyn marched in. "What is this?" she demanded, meaning my uncle.

Alex was wheezing harder, looking more pale and skeletal, looking and sounding distinctly like something the cats dragged in off the street.

"You're not supposed to be here," she said. "Nobody is supposed to be here. How did you get in?"

He just glared at her. His face turned instantly hard, much more unsettling than his physical condition would indicate. He gave me a chill, and I remembered the hard stuff about him that was so easy for me to forget.

"It's okay, Mrs. Llewelleyn," Callum George said.

"He's my uncle," I said.

"Well . . ." She was noticeably shifting away from him now. "He's still not to be in here. He has to go right now."

He got right to his feet, did a small half wobble, then went rigid so not to let her see. Then, silently, he walked toward the other guys. He reached into his pocket, pulled out some bills.

He shook Callum's hand, thanked him, then gave him ten dollars.

"Whoa, Mr. Bishop, I can't take this from you."

"Yes, you can," Alex said sternly, warmly. "You played music for the public, me, and you should be paid for it. Now you have had your first paying gig and it's only up from here. Maybe a little sideways, too, but then up. How does it feel?"

Callum stared at the bill, then at Alex. "It feels very good, actually."

Alex laughed quick and hard. Made himself cough. "I was a busker myself for years. Made pennies playing in the streets, but the pennies added up. And I was getting paid to play music, which was beautiful. But you earn it. Even went to the Busking World Championships in Halifax, Nova Scotia, and did pretty well, too. Time of my life."

He moved on to Neil, repeated the gesture, repeated the phrase, "Time of my life." He went on to Tobias Kolb, who made a tentative move to hand the money back.

Alex pointed at him. "It's true money can't buy you happiness. But it can rent it for a good while. So go on."

Tobias grinned shyly and took it.

"Same goes for love," Alex added, "in case you were wondering."

Then he was on to me, passing Llewellyn on the way and looking at her in an I-dare-you kind of way.

He paid me the going rate. I knew better than to resist. And anyway he looked so happy. So beat and happy.

I never much minded before, not having the dad.

I minded now.

This, I think, was what I was afraid of.

"Are we doing something later?" I said.

"Afraid I'm too wrecked now," he said through a whistly sigh.

"Me too, actually," I said. "Tomorrow?"

"Tomorrow absolutely," he said, and kissed me on the cheek.

I was stunned. I was okay.

"Right," Mrs. Llewellyn shouted as soon as he was gone, "I want to hear 'Mandy,' and it better be good."

We gave her "Mandy." And it was better than good.

8

Lost and Found

He stood me up.

"Where is he, Ma? He was supposed to be here. We were going to do something. We were going to do something yesterday and then he wasn't up to it, then we were going to do something today and he just doesn't show."

Ma was trying hard to come up with something, but what did she know? She had no more control over this than I did, and I was making it harder by sitting in the front window staring out and pouting like a kid waiting for Saturday Dad when Saturday Dad wasn't coming.

"Not that I care," I said, completing the pathetic picture.

She came up behind me and started kneading my neck muscles like bread dough.

"You know how I feel about that neck rubbing," I said sternly.

"I know," she said. She continued rubbing, because we both knew how I felt about it.

"I realize it's difficult, Elvin. You never asked for this."

"I never asked for this," I said.

"I try to talk to him, but it doesn't change it. He has to keep himself to himself, for whatever reasons of his own. He wants to come close, but only so close. Like a wolf coming to the backyard."

"Precisely," I said. "And it was his idea. I never wanted to be bothered by any of this. It was his idea. And then he goes and stands me up."

"He's done worse things," she said, digging her thumbs in a little deeper.

"Ow," I said.

"Sorry."

"I never asked for this, Ma."

"I know you didn't."

"Not that I care."

"Not that you do, no." She gave my muscles a last firm squeeze, then clapped me on the shoulders and kissed me on the ear. She left then to go and make my supper, which she hadn't expected to have to make.

And left me there sitting in the window like a dope. Like a five-year-old dope.

I wasn't even thinking of him anymore. By the next day he had disappeared entirely from my consciousness, just as quickly as he had shown up.

I could do that. That was one of my best skills, so if I needed Alex Bishop to have never been there, then he never was.

So I was genuinely surprised when I walked through the door on Sunday after the movies and found my uncle's bones spread across my sofa, and my dog licking his unconscious head.

"You're late," I said.

His eyes opened slowly. "I'm sorry."

"Is that the best you can do?" I asked, and yes, I heard myself. I had gone from acting like his kid to acting like his spouse in forty-eight hours as my sense of identity was ripped to shreds.

"I wasn't feeling well yesterday or the day before, Elvin. I am sorry. Can we forget it? You shouldn't dwell on stuff, especially negative stuff. Do your best living in the now, and your later will be a little less messed up."

He sat up, and looked like he regretted it.

"You don't look too good still."

"I always look like this when I wake up."

"I saw you wake up on the couch once before and it didn't look like this."

"I haven't felt the same since I winded myself on the tuba."

"That's a new one. I've had my playing turn other people green before, but never myself."

157

"Well, I wasn't trained in the instrument like you. It'll pass. Where's your mom?"

"She's stealing some overtime."

"I still got to talk to her about how easy it is to break in here. You guys should move someplace nicer."

"Well, we're comfortable, and the rent's reasonable, and since you're the only career criminal with any interest in the place . . . I think we'll be okay."

"Hmm. Well, we'll see. Anyway, looks like it's just the Bishop men then. Can I take you for an early supper?"

As days out go, I had to admit a restaurant sure sounded more tempting than a sweatbox.

"I suppose," I said.

"This is my favorite restaurant," Alex said.

"I never ate Thai food before. And how did a restaurant half a mile from my house get to be your favorite restaurant without my ever meeting you before?"

"Like I said, I've been hanging around."

It seemed like a nice place to be hanging around if you were going to be hanging around. Lots of gold and green and leather in the walls, the ceilings, and the furniture. The smells were all warm, spices I didn't know. Some music—one instrument, something between a mandolin and a harpsichord—played in the background so quietly it might have just been coming out of my own head. And best of all we were there in the between hours, well after lunch but before prime dinnertime, so we had the place to ourselves.

"I always come at this hour," Alex said. "It is the only time for eating out."

"I think there are other times," I said. "But this is pretty great."

"Did I ever tell you that it's really your mother's fault that I was in prison all that time?"

"No, actually, you didn't."

"Didn't I? Well, here it goes. . . ."

Just then the waiter arrived. Alex knew him, and vice versa.

"Hey Jerry," he said.

"Hello, Mr. Bishop."

He didn't look like a Jerry to me, so maybe he was just humoring my uncle.

"Listen, Elvin, if you're new at this, it's smart to go with the tod mun and the pad thai. Can't go wrong."

"I'll have the tod mun and the pad thai," I said, having no interest in going wrong.

"The *special* pad thai," Alex insisted. "And for me, I'll just have the old standard. And Jerry, hit the spices. I mean, hit those spices. Hurt us, Jerry, is what I'm saying."

"Pain it is," Jerry said, scribbling. "And to drink?"

"We'll have some tea please, and some orange juice. And a bottle of Tsingtao."

"Mr. Bishop? I thought you weren't drinking beer?"

"Oh, that's not for me. It's for my nephew here."

"He is old enough?"

"Oh yes. Of course."

Jerry cocked an eyebrow at me, scribbled some more, then left us.

"So I was fourteen at the beginning of the week. I was sixteen at the gym. And now I'm legal drinking age. I'm aging at a frightening pace."

"Join the club, pal," he said seriously.

"I never liked clubs very much. My mother did not put you in jail."

"Okay, not exactly. But she should have. And the fact that she didn't has caused me endless trouble. See, when I stole all that money off you and your mom—remember we told you about that?"

"Oh, let me think . . . stole money, stole money . . ."

"Ya. Well your mother, being too damn good. Being too damn good for her own damn good, refused to pursue the thing and put me in the can where I frankly belonged. So I said to myself, after about half a second of some very unproductive soul-searching, I said, hey, that didn't hurt so much. Matter of fact, that didn't hurt one little bit. So I went out and scammed somebody else.

And that didn't hurt either, 'cause I didn't even get caught. Then, being pretty good with figures and bad with conscience, I built up a nice little hobby, thank you very much, of jerking people's money off them without them even noticing."

Jerry came and set the drinks down.

"Until somebody noticed," I said.

"Until somebody noticed," he said.

I reached for my cup of tea. Alex reached for his.

He went on. "Then I was good and caught. The lady who caught me caught me thoroughly, and she turned out to be not even remotely as sweet-natured and forgiving as your mom. Funny enough, neither did all the other folks who caught wind and started catching on to my earlier acts of skulduggery. So the short and the long of it is that I went to jail, for a lot of thieving and for a very long time. Whereas, if your mother had only done the right thing in the first place and turned me in, it would have been my first offense, and a lot less money, so I would have been treated a lot more leniently and I would have learned my lesson and not done it again. So as you can see, your mother is, of course, very much responsible for much of the hard times that have befallen me in this life. Were it not for her, I would have been a different man altogether."

A funny sensation had come over me at some point

during that statement from my uncle. It was not unlike the brain-boiling, eye-swimming surrealness of the hotbox sauna experience.

"Excuse me?" I said. I sounded just like Clint Eastwood when I said it. I even squinted.

A sly grin slipped across Alex's face. He knew what he was doing. Did he know why, was the question.

"And I would have killed myself," he added just as Jerry set the food down in front of us.

"You would not," I insisted, and took a bite of one of my dishes, the one shaped like fish cakes.

"Yes, I would, Elvin, believe it. But it wouldn't have been the dramatic way. It would have been the Bishop way, gradually over time. Would have killed myself with my appetites. With the smoke and the drink and the drugs, with the food, and the fun, and the foolishness."

"What," I said, with my mouth now filled with the second cake which turned out to be luscious, "are you saying you *liked* prison? That prison was a good place, and it made you such a great guy?"

"No, I didn't like it. But it was a good place, for me. It was the right place, for me. My father never reached my age. His father never reached my age. Your father, never reached my age. And it all started changing for me in jail. I lost and found all the important things while I was inside. I lost my weight, and my thirst, and my crazy compulsiveness. I found discipline, I found respect, and I found God, none of which I had before I went in. It was miraculous."

"An embarrassment of riches," I said, kind of smart mouth.

"No, more of an embarrassment of embarrassments, but you don't necessarily need to hear about all those. What you do need to hear about is how I came out of there knowing I owed you guys, you and your mom, even more than I owed you before. And even though it took me some time to work up the guts to get here, I'm here to tell you thanks. Thanks, and a whole lot more than thanks."

I kept eating all through his talk, staring at him, then at my food, then away altogether. Then at him.

"You're welcome," I said tentatively.

Alex reached for my bottle of beer.

"Hey," I said.

He frowned. "You didn't think this was for you, did you? You're not old enough."

"So why didn't you just order it for yourself?"

"Hush," Alex said, "it's Jerry. He likes to watch my health."

Quickly Alex took a long, hard drink from the bottle, then slipped it back in front of me. "Ahhh," he said, with real satisfaction. "Sometimes it's really nice, having somebody to take an interest in your well-being." He stopped there, sat back, looked away, and listened to his own words. "Yes, sometimes, it is really, really nice, to have somebody caring for your well-being. But then sometimes you have to get away from it too."

He looked back at me then, after the words were gone, and smiled. Then it flattened out again, like the corners of his mouth were too heavy to hold up for very long.

"So then let's do that," I said. "Let's take a look at your well-being."

"All right, let's do. You know how I had the diabetes, but that's under control now. Then there was the cancer from the sugar substitutes, but that's gone, too, along with my toes, and a couple of other things that I really didn't need anyway. You'll find that as you get older, that really we're like them rockets they shoot off into space. They get up there and don't need the extra parts, fuel tanks, and whatnot they needed at the beginning. So things can start dropping off you, and you don't really miss them."

He smiled again. Then he stole the rest of the beer.

"I have to say, you do seem to have a knack for taking the bright side, Uncle Alex."

He pointed at me like a teacher. Like an old teacher. "I do, Elvin, you know, I do. I never had that when I was young, but I do now, and I'm making sure I enjoy the crap out of it from here on. Right, like, here's one. Cancer. Bright side . . ."

"It *has* a bright side."

"Yup. For me it does, anyhow. I was in this bar. I was out of jail, I had reformed and all . . . but I was still relearning. How to *be*, you know. One step forward, one step back kind of thing. So I was having one of my one steps back. And so I got into a bit of a bust up, which I used to do back when."

"You were a fighter? You look like *I* could take you. And if you knew how much of an insult that was, you'd probably hit me with a chair right now."

"I was a fighter. Remember, I used to be notably bigger. But more importantly, I was a veteran. Of the fighting. And that's the key. I wasn't any world champion, but the thing about me was, I had been hit. A lot. Now, a thing happens to a guy when he gets hit a lot. . . ."

Alex signaled for another beer. Jerry came over. "This for you?" he asked.

"Not for me, no," Alex said.

"Then why you raising your hand? Why not him?"

Alex looked at him, which was me. He stared and waited.

And waited.

I was not raising my hand. I did not want a beer. Why would I be raising my hand?

Alex, a man with apparently no time for wasting, reached over and helped me raise my hand.

Jerry made a disapproving groan, but went off to get the beer anyway.

"I'd like a Diet Coke?" I called after him.

"So, I was saying, when you get hit a lot like I did, something happens to you."

"Ya," I said, "you get *hurt*. Even I know that."

"No. You *stop* getting hurt. You stop caring whether you get hit or not, and you concentrate on taking a piece out of the other guy. That, my friend, is when a guy becomes very scary indeed. That, is what I was. Scary. Tough."

"Nuts," I said, filling my mouth with noodles.

"Nuts is right," Alex said. "And coincidentally, that brings us back to my story. I was in this fight, in this bar, when the guy takes a wild flying whack at mine. Nuts, that is. With them big pointy ol' cowboy boots. And scores a direct hit."

I put my fork down, and rested my hands in my lap. My Diet Coke came, along with the beer. I rested the Diet Coke in my lap.

"I see you're uncomfortable there," Alex said, clearly relishing the job at hand. "But fear not. That is where cancer's good side came in."

I waited. He grinned. Seemed to take about three hours.

"'Cause I don't have any. Nuts. They had to come off, some time back, surgically. Replaced 'em with these rubbery fakes. The super balls, I called them. So the guy punts me right up the middle, and while it surely did hurt—kind of like getting punched in the armpit—it didn't hurt anything like it was supposed to. So I played it up, and played it so cool, just put my fists on my hips like Superman and scowled at the guy. I have to be a little bit immodest here and say, it was quite a moment for me.

"He was impressed. He backed away. Then just went back to the bar. Which was good, because the guy was stomping me up till then, and would have continued to do so until probably I was dead. I wasn't a good fighter anymore, you see.

"So cancer saved my life."

Maybe it was his story, or maybe it was something in the air, since I was sitting there with my mouth hanging open, but I started feeling a flashy, burning sensation all around my mouth.

"Ouch," I said. I was speaking to the food and the story together.

"Want to try mine?" he said.

"Have *you* tried yours?" I said because I knew he hadn't.

"I'm getting to it," he said. "You want a taste?"

"You have any diseases I might actually catch?"

"Don't think so," he said, and extended a spoonful of his white, chunky soup.

I took it.

"Nothing contagious since the prison doc killed off the last of the syphilis and the leprosy."

You know that thing, where you already have something in your mouth, then you get grossed out before you can manage to swallow?

I held the soup in my mouth, struggling, thinking what to do.

Till the soup decided for me.

"Yeow," I said, after I had involuntarily swallowed the flaming ball of liquid.

"I know," he said, "it is fantastic stuff." Then he took a big sip of the beer. Oh no, he took a complete, draining slug of the beer. "I usually don't eat anyplace else."

"Or here, either," I said.

"Aw, I'm just not starving right now, that's all."

"Starving is actually what you do look like," I said. "Eat your food."

"That's nice," Alex said. "That is so nice, you worrying about me. Thank you."

"I'm not worrying," I said, picking up my fork in order to change the subject. Then with two more quick, spicy bites, I had finished my whole meal without his taking any of his.

"You really should pace yourself more, Elvin," he said. "You know, I look at you and frankly, I gotta say you are the perfect recipe for a Dead Bishop."

"You wanting a Dead Bishop, Mr. Bishop?" Jerry was back, and speaking from underneath a big frown.

"No, Jerry, sorry, I was just talking about something else."

"What's he talking about?" I asked. "Is that something you can order here? A Dead Bishop?"

Alex got a kind of whimsical, faraway look on his face. "You know, Jerry, now that you mention it . . ."

"No," Jerry said. "And I didn't mention it, you did."

"Aw, go on, make me a Dead Bishop."

"What's a Dead Bishop?" I asked nervously.

"This is," Jerry said, pointing with both hands at my uncle, "if he doesn't behave himself."

"It's a drink, Elvin," Alex said in a soft, calm, serene, creepy voice. "It's a lovely, lovely drink. I invented it. It has green tea in it."

"It has *everything* in it," Jerry insisted.

"Ya, ya," Alex said warmly, as if this were a good thing.

He didn't finish his soup. I finished his soup. He finished two Dead Bishops instead. I had coconut ice cream for desert. It was about the creamiest ice cream I ever ate, and just what my tongue needed. Alex had a bite. He started looking very tired before the check came. Then he pulled out his gold credit card and paid.

"What are you doing, Alex?" I said.

"Call me Dad, wouldja?"

"No, I wouldjn't," I said.

"Oh. Then call me Uncle Alex, at least. Could you do that for me?"

"I could, yes. What are you doing, Uncle Alex?"

"Ah that's nice. Could you say it again?"

"What are you *doing*, Uncle Alex?" I snapped.

"Paying the bill."

"No. I mean, I thought you didn't drink anymore?"

"No, but I don't drink any less, either." He could barely get the words out before busting up with big, fat guffaws of laughter. "I love when I get to say that," he said.

And he guffawed a little more. Then he laughed. Then chuckled, grunted, then stopped. Next I knew, his head dipped, his chin hit his chest, and he went into mumbling, slurring, spluttering weak, unintelligible sounds to himself.

"Alex?" I said. Then I reached across to shake him. "Alex?"

He didn't respond. Even the noises stopped as he went limp in my hand. Then when I sat back, he sat forward, flopping onto the table.

I looked around, stupid and helpless. "Jerry," I called, like I was calling my own mother rather than a Thai waiter I had met less than an hour ago.

But he was there. On the scene, on the case, and prepared.

"Come on, Mr. Bishop," Jerry said, picking my uncle right up off the table roughly. He kept talking to him and jostling him about as he stuffed chocolate-covered cookies into his mouth. "Come on, Mr. Bishop," Jerry said, louder and more motherly. "Chew now. Chew for me. How many of my customers actually make me do the chewing for them now? You are a very lazy customer, Mr. Bishop. Come on now. . . ."

He was great. Jerry was great. I had never seen a waiter act like this before. I could not have imagined anybody acting like this before. Taking care of a man, like he was a helpless baby. Like he was his own helpless baby. I would have figured somebody acting like my uncle was acting would get thrown out of a restaurant, rather than cared for, and I was thoroughly embarrassed by it all, to be honest.

"Sorry," I said as Jerry simmered down a little and Alex simmered up.

"Sorry for what?" Jerry asked. "What did you do?"

"Nothing. Sorry . . . for all this."

"Oh well, it happens. You should have made him eat,

though. He must eat. The blood sugar gets too low . . . happens just like that."

"It's happened before?"

"Oh yes. Fortunately, he was not my first diabetic. We have quite a few regulars. Guess we got some kind of reputation. Come here for the service. I think he does this on purpose, though, to get the free cookies."

"I do not," Alex said sternly. He was wide awake now, and slumped sideways in Jerry's grip. Like a fighter who'd just been counted out and was being treated by his cornerman. "I can pay for my own cookies. They weren't even that good." He straightened up, a little wobbly, but a new man compared to a few minutes earlier.

"What do you think"—Jerry laughed—"I break out the fresh cookies for the seizures?" He gave Alex a friendly pat on the shoulder before walking away. "And no more Dead Bishops," he said.

"No," Alex said sheepishly, staring across at me with a bit of a blush rising in his cheeks.

"I thought you said you didn't have the diabetes anymore?" I felt like I could be bossy and angry and parental now, so I went with it.

"I don't, but I don't have it any less," he said with a smaller laugh. "It came back, I guess. Won't happen again."

I felt my brows knitting together. Felt like a lot of

work. I couldn't understand why parental types were so fond of it. "About what percent of the time would you say you tell the truth, Alex?"

"Would I say? I would say one hundred percent. That's what I would say."

I did ask.

"That was scary, Alex," I said.

"*Uncle* Alex."

"No." I was still feeling too parental. I'd say the cycle was complete now.

He must have noticed, because he got all juvenile. His head sunk to his chin again, but I could tell by the almost lifelike way he held his body that it wasn't a seizure this time.

"Hey," I snapped.

He looked up. And caught me five hundred miles off my guard.

His eyes were loose in their sockets, like they were some tiny child's eyes shoved into his full-grown head. And they were swimming, floating in all that space, in all that red space.

I didn't want to see this. Nobody wants to see this. You don't want to see babies or girls or crybabies cry, people who are supposed to cry, never mind adult jailbird people who are not supposed to. Not if you have a heart, you don't want to see that, and even if he is not full-on crying you don't want to see it, don't want to see crying or anything related to crying, which this was.

And you don't ever want to see yourself crying or anything like crying, which is exactly what is likely to happen if you have anything like a heart and you are exposed to anything like the wrong people crying.

"Uncle, okay? Uncle. There, uncle. Uncle Alex. I don't see why you have to be reminded, anyway. That's what you are. It's not as if I can fire you or demote you or rip some stripes off your arm now, is it? You went away for a million years, lied and stole and hid and God knows what else, and then came back and *poof* there you were, all *uncle* on me anyway. So you don't really need to be that insecure, do you? The job is yours. You are my uncle, okay? It's a job for life, like a judge or Tom Jones or something, so relax. You are my uncle."

Through it all I kept looking down and away and back at *Uncle* Alex's liquid eyes to check for signs of progress or complete screwing up. I found—of course, because life is so hysterically funny and unfair and inconclusive— signs of both. A weak smile was making its way like a lost wagon train across his lower face, while the waterworks only increased up there at the top.

"Will you go someplace with me?"

I couldn't decide whether to be worried or frustrated. I'd most likely get around to both.

"I *am* someplace with you," I said, pointing at the other tables with place settings and cloth napkins and wineglasses. "And the other day, I was at another someplace with you." I raised my mighty right arm, rolled up my sleeve, and pointed at my brand-new hulking biceps. It looked okay, as long as you didn't poke it with a finger.

"A different someplace," he said, graciously nodding approval at my muscle. "I want to take you to see somebody."

It set off bells. My mother suggested once that she wanted me to *see somebody*. I knew what that meant.

"I'm not crazy," I said. "I'm just big boned."

He stared at me in such a bemused way, I thought he was maybe slipping into another seizure.

"Oh, you are crazy, Elvin," he said, rising carefully but steadily from his seat, "but we're not going to see somebody for you, we're going to see somebody for me. And I need you there."

Alex didn't wait for a response, just headed on out of the restaurant. I followed. Wasn't like I was going to argue with him, was I? He needed me. He needed something anyway, someone, that was for sure. And for right now I was that something.

He had succeeded in this much, whether he was trying to or not: he had made me feel pretty important. And that didn't happen every day.

"Alex," I said as I caught up to him out on the street, "are you talking about now? Are we going to meet somebody now?"

"I'd like to," he said, and I could hear the old wheezing like when he'd winded himself on the tuba, "but I'm not going to be up to it. Stamina . . . seems to be becoming . . . more of a problem."

"Sure," I said, "fine. Whenever."

"Whenever is tomorrow. Tomorrow is whenever, Elvin."

"Okay," I said, and walked along right beside him, not touching him, but being handy just in case.

He seemed steady enough by the time we reached my house. But not so steady I wasn't nervous. "You want to come in?" I asked.

He just shook his head.

"Why not? Come see Ma."

He didn't seem to like that idea at all. He looked embarrassed, looking down, looking away, shuffling his feet. He shook his head more vigorously.

"That's just foolish," I said, and mounted the stairs. "But just wait here so she can say hi."

As I was unlocking the door, I looked back over my shoulder and he was already gone.

9
Whenever

"So who do you figure he wants you to meet?" Frankie asked over Monday lunch. "Criminals? I bet he wants to introduce you to his underworld syndicate, to break you into the game. That's what he came back for. That's been his plan all along, to pass along the family business. This is the coolest thing I ever heard. You are going to be a big muck, Elvin. I mean, the actual crime stuff might not be such a nice thing . . . but the suits you're going to wear, and the money, and the power . . ."

I just stared, gape mouthed. He was sitting next to me, his face inches from mine, and I just stared. I couldn't even stare the old stare at the moment, I was so blown away. I couldn't tell whether I was more stunned by the lunatic outlandishness of Frank's tale, or the horrifying possibility it might be true.

As usual, it was down to Mikie to tip the balance. He finished placing the individual black olive slices evenly around the inside of his tuna sandwich, patted the whole wheat top back on, then turned to Frank.

"I'll give you a buck if you shut up," Mike said.

"Hey, it's my theory, that's all."

"Didn't I tell you not to have any more theories? You only wind up hurting yourself when you have a theory. Unless your theory involves hair or hair products, you're on shaky ground."

"I don't care; I'm sticking by my theory."

"I couldn't even begin to think who he would want me to meet," I said. "It's been making me kind of crazy today. At first I was okay, but then I realized anything's possible here. Alex is a total wild card. Then I started thinking, when I was lying in bed this morning at, like, five, half awake—"

"Uh-oh," Mike said, "the spook hours . . ."

"The spook hours is right," I said. "I was lying there, shaking, convinced that today Alex was going to bring me to meet my father. Ya, that it would turn out that he wasn't dead either, and that was what this was all about and I swear, guys, I don't know what I'd do. I swear, I'd go mental and a half. I never got back to sleep. And it just kept getting worse and worse."

It was Frank's turn to stare gape mouthed at me. "Holy smokes," he said.

Mike was required to put down his sandwich again, which he does not appreciate once he has begun his methodical deconstruction of his meal. He reached across the table and grabbed both of my forearms tightly.

"Your dad is dead, El. I promise."

"Really?"

"Ya."

"Thanks."

My reassurance lasted about four seconds.

"How do you know for sure?"

"Easy," he said. "Your ma. She'd let Alex be pretend dead. But . . . no way. Not to you. Not her. No way."

Because he was Mikie, because he was so supremely reasonable and so magnificently sure of my mother's fineness, there was only one way to treat this.

I was calling my mother.

I pulled my phone out of my bag, in the face of ferocious protests from my two oldest and best friends. Because this was seriously against the rules here. Setting fires was a less punishable offense than a student using a mobile phone between the hours of eight and two. At the stroke of two, the place sounds like a gigantic music box.

"Ma," I said as my bodyguards frantically scanned the perimeter for faculty goons.

"Elvin?" she said. "What a sweet . . . wait a minute, are you in trouble? It's only lunchtime and you shouldn't—"

"Ma, is Dad dead?"

She was at her best when she was overly cool.

"Pardon me?"

"I'm kind of freaking, Ma. Thinking Alex is going to bring me to meet Dad. I can't shake it. Is Dad dead?"

There was too, too long a pause on the other end. Maybe a second and a half.

"Hold on, hon," she said, "let me check. Hmm, hmm, yes, I do believe he is deceased."

To some people that might have sounded horrible. To me it was the highest art of mothering. If she treated this with anything other than snap, I would have gone into convulsions of anxiety.

"Thanks," I said.

"Boy, you don't trust me with anything," she said. "What did you think, I had misplaced him? Did you think maybe the past decade or so was one spectacular surprise party for you but we were waiting for just that right moment for him to jump out of the closet?"

I felt like eating my lunch, finally. I also felt like listening to her tinny phone voice for a good long time now. "Thanks—" I said but was cut short by the sharp kicking of Mike's feet under the table and Frank, first elbowing me and then leaning right over on top of me. Then he snatched the phone right off my ear.

"Hey," I said.

"Hey yourself," barked Mrs. Llewellyn from behind me.

I looked up to see her glowering, first at me, then Frank. Frank gestured to her with the one-finger, hold-on-a-sec move, which turned her face plum.

"Okay," Frank said into the phone. "That's right. No, don't worry about it. All set. Sure. Oh, you too. Love ya, baby. 'Bye."

I would have paid good money to hear both sides of that conversation.

"What are you doing?" Mrs. Llewellyn demanded.

"Sorry, it was an important call. I had to handle a crisis."

"I could have sworn I saw Mr. Bishop talking on that phone from across the cafeteria."

"No ma'am," Frank said, going all soft and wasting his considerable charm on her.

"Oh really?" she said. "Well, that is not even your phone, Francis. Everyone knows your phone is the famous silver-plated phone."

Franko looked around a bit before answering and I feared he was lost. I needn't have feared.

"Not to brag or anything, Mrs. Llewellyn, but if you're me you gotta have two of these things, minimum."

Not sure what the word was for the shade just past plum, but I certainly now knew what it looked like. She wrote out the little pink slip while growling lowly, then stuck it in Franko's hand.

"I'll see you in detention this afternoon," she said. Then she grabbed my phone away from him.

"Wow," Mike and I both said when it was safe to speak again. I added, "Thanks, Frank. Really. You didn't need to do that."

"Ah," he said, looking utterly unconcerned, "you have a big date this afternoon."

"Well . . . wait, so do you."

"Ya, but for you it's rare."

We may have had the most unfathomable three-way relationship in the vicinity, but at the moment I didn't mind if we ever figured it out. I sort of hoped we didn't.

This time Alex was on the ball. He was at the school gate—safely outside it—when I got there.

"Okay," I said. "I'm ready, almost."

"Almost?"

"I decided I can't go seeing anybody like this. I don't want to be an embarrassment to either of us. I have to do one thing before I go see anybody."

"What did you do?" Sal demanded when I walked in the door, past his twisting red-and-white candy cane barber pole thing. He was so mad he got up out of his chair. "I spent all these years taking care of your head, and you go behind my back and get this?" He patted the top of my admittedly bouncy head like he was dribbling a well-overinflated basketball. "Who did this to you?" he demanded.

"Hello, Sal," I said.

He stopped. He regained his old-world manners without relinquishing his current fury. "Hello, Mr. Sponge Head. Get in the chair."

"This is my uncle Alex," I said.

"Hello, Uncle Alex," Sal said. "Did you do this to him?"

Alex laughed. "I am happy to say I did not. I thought he looked fine before. You do good work."

"Right," Sal said, pointing up at Alex's own dodgy head. "You just wait, I'll take care of you after the emergency."

"He was trying to look like his pal Frank—"

"Of course, the golden retriever."

"That's him."

"I was not."

"He's kind of fixated on him right now."

"I am not."

"Stop squirming. You wanna be stabbed with the scissors? Anyway, this was supposed to look like your friend? Your friend maybe after he was dragged backward through an electrical fence."

"Sorry, Sal."

He was gracious about it, though.

"Yes, well, sorry doesn't make it better. What am I supposed to do with this now?"

My uncle came to the rescue.

"There's only one thing you can do for it," he said solemnly.

"I fear you are correct," Sal said, matching the tone.

"What?" I said, then, "No . . . no . . ."

Alex came closer, so the three of us were now facing me in the mirror. "It's gotten worse."

"It has not," I insisted, mortified at the unthinkable thought that I knew to be true.

"It has, since we went in the pool. The chlorine's got at it now. And it's like it's still working on you right now, 'cause every day it's a little fuzzier."

"Dear God," I said, and leaned a little closer, dangerously closer, to the mirror.

I realized I had somehow managed to ignore my physical self for the last few days. I had not seen the grisly process still going on up at the peak of Mt. Me.

I sat there in the chair, up in the air since Sal still insisted on pumping the chair up like he always had, even though he had to get up on his toes to do his work now. And with the black leatherette apron buttoned right up tight to my neck, I looked like a grotesquely overgrown version of those Christmas angels we used to make in school by stapling a sheet of construction paper into a cone and sticking a Styrofoam ball on top. Only without the wings. And black instead of white. And in place of the little Styrofoam ball, a pink grapefruit.

And the hair itself had reached that miracle color where orange and green somehow become related.

I believe I spoke for everyone when I gasped.

"Oh goodness, don't cry, Elvin," Sal said, clipping away big clumps to make me happy.

"I am not crying. It's that hair tonic stuff, always irritates my eyes."

"You sure it's not the mirror irritating your eyes?" Alex joked.

"You should talk. At least in a few minutes, I'm going to be cured."

"Touché," Alex said, and retreated to a guest chair and a tabloid newspaper.

A surprisingly short time later, it was done. And gone.

"I'm bald now," I said rather calmly.

"Not bald," Sal lied, rather baldly.

"Wow," Alex said.

"Not bald at all," Sal said. "Look, up close here, you can see." He pulled up behind me with a large, handheld mirror, beaming the reflection of the fat bald back of my head off the mirror in front of me and back to my disbelieving eyes. "See?" he said, working heroically to grip something hairlike at my skull between his thumb and index finger. I felt a little pinch up there. "I was able to save some seed hair, where the color and texture was still your own. All the bad has been weeded away now."

This seemed like a good time to let my well-developed gift for fantasy, delusion, and nonsense take over.

"All the bad has been weeded away now," I repeated robotically. I even allowed myself a frigid and vacant smile, until my reflection frightened me and I had to give that up.

"That's right," Sal said.

"All the bad," I said wistfully. "All the bad has been weeded away. There is no bad left, of any kind. It's like a magic haircut. You are a magic haircutter, Sal. I knew I should have come here all along."

I was letting my eyes close as I drifted into the pleasant other world I call "the place without the mirrors," when somebody ruined it.

"Har," Alex laughed loudly, jolting me before stuffing a knuckle into his mouth.

"All right," I said, jumping up and removing my bib. "That's you. In the chair, bub."

"Okay," he said, still chuckly.

When Alex was settled in and buttoned up, Sal stood, then walked around him, taking it in from angles. He went right up and sort of patted Alex's head a few times, then stood back, as if he expected it to blow or something.

"So what happened to you?" Sal asked.

"Well, it kind of got set on fire a couple of times. Never really quite came back right after that."

"Hmm," Sal said, "Are you sure you two are supposed to be out by yourselves?"

"Not sure," Alex said, giving me a big mirror grin. "But here we are."

"So what do you want me to do?"

Alex continued looking at me, and I at him.

"I think there's only one thing for it," he said.

10
Whenever (cont'd.)

We stood there on the sidewalk staring at each other's heads.

"You didn't have to do that," I said.

"Solidarity dictated that I did."

"Well, whoever Sol is, he's no friend of yours."

Alex rubbed his hand back and forth over his skull for the fiftieth time already. I did the same thing, again. It was like yawning.

"No great loss in either case, though, huh?"

"I suppose not."

We walked. We got about a block from Sal's when the unthinkable happened.

Not true. It was very thinkable. So thinkable I had been thinking about it since Sal shaved that first bone-colored strip down the right side of my head.

"Hi, guys," I said in such a pathetically fake move-along-nothing-to-see-here voice they didn't even wait a polite second to burst out laughing.

"For God's *sake*, Elvin," Frankie said, pointing at my dome.

"Are you trying to make Grog feel pretty?" Mikie asked. And the two of them fell over themselves laughing.

I almost hated to interrupt. "What are you doing out of detention?" I asked Frank.

"Oh, well, your pal Llewellyn turns out to be such a power-nuts control freak, she won't let this go. She's determined to solve the case. So she cuts me a deal, that if I admit to her that it was your phone, she gets her satisfaction, I get points for loyalty, and nobody gets detention. Sweet, no?"

"Hmm," I said. "Sweet, she isn't. But fine. Where's my phone?"

"She says you have to come get it from her yourself."

Ah, there it is.

"And I have to tell you, I'm not completely sure about that last part, about nobody getting detention. 'Cause right after I 'fessed, she stood there pounding her fist into her palm and going, 'Right. Bishop. Bishop.'"

"Hey," I said. "You sold me out. I thought you were taking the hit for me?"

"That was for today. Because you had something to do. And if I knew that what you had to do was go out and turn yourselves into a pair of boobs, I might have thought twice about it in the first place. To save you from your boob self."

I heard next to me the sound of my uncle working up a furious wheeze. I looked, to find it was furious indeed.

"Have you had about enough of this crap from these guys, Elvin?" he growled. His voice took on a whole new, scary tone I wouldn't think his body could produce. His face screwed down into a nasty scowl that changed his expression, his age, even his size into something altogether different. His face started getting deep red, then it spread to his head and, of course, the new scalp design didn't help.

"Well, I kind of have. But I had had enough a few years ago, and I didn't do much about it then, either. And this time I have to admit they have a pretty good point. I have not been kind to my head."

"Oh, for cripes . . ." He wasn't too impressed with my position. So he took matters into his own hands. "You two need to just shut your holes. You making fun of this guy? Well, let me tell you something. There's a lot more to this boy than you think. He's been working out, you know." Here Alex had to raise his voice further to be heard above the spluttering.

Why is it that laughter is so much more like yawning than screaming anger is? Why is it that, no matter how unwise an idea it might be at the time, you almost always let yourself get pulled into the laughing fit rather than the fuming anger fit?

"Stop that," Alex snapped at me before going back to them. "He's a lot harder than you think, and it would behoove you to note that."

Did he have to say *behoove*?

"Stop that laughing," Alex demanded. Then, back to the guys. "I'll have you know, this guy here was lifting weights and swimming laps and running the treadmill harder than anybody in the place the other day. And he's got hairier nuts, I'll bet, than the two of you put together. I know, I've seen them."

Oh God.

"That tears it," Alex said as the two of them dropped to their knees, right there on the sidewalk, dying before our eyes with joy. You couldn't blame them except for the fact that this was such not the right time.

I managed to stop laughing myself at the point where my uncle started praising my hairy bits.

"Can we just go?" I said quietly, tugging on Alex's arm.

"No, we certainly cannot go. Where is your pride, boy?"

It went thataway, was the first of a thousand wise guy/honest guy answers that flew through my mind. But I didn't get a chance since Frankie was much more anxious to help out.

"It's in his jockstrap," he called out.

Alex could take no more. His head appeared to be inflating, with the blood that was pumping to it.

"Elvin," he said through gritted teeth, "kick his ass."

Oh God.

"Elvin!" he snapped when he noticed I wasn't kicking anything.

"Oh, come on," I said. I whined, actually. "Why would I want to do that?"

Mikie cut in, "I don't know, El, think about it: Frankie's ass."

Here's how much Silly Putty is in my head. Because he told me to think about it, I thought about it.

"Hey," I snapped, much, much too late. They were laughing harder than ever. You could hardly blame them. I was a figure of fun, seemingly programmed to behave only in ways that would make them laugh.

My uncle was staring at me now, with his hands on his hips and his head just about ready for liftoff. A nasty mix of amazement and disgust had settled on his face like the mud splash from a speeding car. "You can't just let people make fun of you like that," he said.

"I don't know," I said. "I'm doing a pretty good job so far."

It occurred to me that while Alex and I may have shared some genetic material, we did not fully share my sense of humor. Or his sense of outrage.

"I am sorely tempted, sir," my uncle said, "to kick your ass myself."

Which, I think, changed the tone of things somewhat. Good options were pretty scarce from what I could tell.

"Come on, Alex. I don't want to fight. Nobody here wants to fight."

Bastard. Rotten, rotten bastard. Sorry for the outburst, but you'll see what I mean.

"I do," Frankie said brightly.

"See, there you go," Alex said.

"I am not fighting anybody," I said. "This is completely stupid."

See, the thing was, they didn't take Alex seriously. They didn't believe he could possibly want this to happen, so they just ran with it and in the process wound my uncle up into a frenzy.

"Let's get it on," Frank said.

Thing was, here is the sweet irony of it. And by sweet irony I mean, as most people do, *what crap*. Frankie was, by his behavior, making me want to fight. I was getting madder and madder, and I was sure my own newly shiny skull was giving me away like a barometer.

But I would rise above.

"No," I said coolly, though cool I was not.

"No?" Frank said, mock disappointed.

"*No?*" Alex grunted, homicidally disappointed.

He brushed by me, stomping toward Frank. "See, this is why I'm here," he said. "This is just the type of lesson you have missed without a dad. . . ."

"Oh God, no, Alex!" I shouted.

You may not be surprised to find out that my shout had no noticeable effect.

Alex ran up and locked up with a suddenly worried-looking Frankie. Had to admit the very, very rare sight of a disconcerted Frank was not an unwonderful thing . . . but I couldn't enjoy it for long. He looked at me desperately for help as my enraged uncle grappled with him in a kind of Greco-Roman tango.

"Please stop," I said from pretty far away.

"Hey, really," Mike said, inching up closer to them. "Cut it out. This is really foolish."

"Ya," Frank said.

"Shut up," Alex barked. "Not so tough now, huh? Not so smart with your mouth now, huh?"

"Well, I didn't think—"

"Shut up," Alex snapped again.

"Well, you *asked* me a question," Frank answered.

I thought it would fizzle out in a few seconds when the players realized how stupid they looked. They didn't; it didn't. Frank, for his part, seemed to be doing a reasonable job of just restraining Alex, who was going at him like Don Quixote at a windmill.

Until Alex grew rapidly, visibly tired. He flailed, struggled. Grappled. Then finally let his arms fall to his sides. Without further incident, Frankie let go of him.

Which was when my ex-con uncle made his move, smacking Frank crisply on the side of his head, snapping that head sideways.

A whole new ballgame. Frankie's face was red, his hair was asymmetrical, and he was serious. He grabbed Alex by the shirt and Alex grabbed him by the shirt and they pushed left and right trying to wrestle each other to the sidewalk.

What I did not expect was Mikie jumping in. He didn't jump in the way rowdies jump into a brawl. But he did jump in seeming to believe Frankie was the one needing help.

"Aw cripes," I said out loud as I scurried over and . . .

Never ever thought I would have need for this combination of words, not in my lifetime, not in any possible context. But here goes:

I jumped in.

I couldn't believe it even as it was happening. The whole crowd of us toppled over like a great, big, idiot sundae. Frankie fell backward with Alex on him, with Mikie on him, with me on him.

It hurt, four guys falling comically, more than you would expect it to.

I took it upon myself to speak for the crowd and shout, "Ouch," when my knuckles first hit the pavement, then my head followed as I rolled off the mound. I reached back to use my new muscles and start pulling jokers out of the pile.

Deep, deep humiliation set in as I had this vision of what was going on. It is a gift I have, a gift given to me by God or Santa or whichever giveth/taketh away being assigns these things out, to keep me from ever getting delusions of grandeur or of dignity. It is the ability/misfortune to actually visually witness myself at the nonsense of my life as if I were a regular paying customer like you, rather than the mere victim of it all. Sometimes I'm blessed enough to see things that aren't even happening in the literal physical sense but only metaphorically like the time I saw clearly the scene of the Last Supper in which all of the apostles were me and at the center was Jesus, holding a brownie way up over his head and making all twelve of me jump for it.

But that was different, though no less humiliating. Here I could see myself and my uncle, with our hysterically glowing heads, fighting it out on the street with my two oldest friends, like a pair of Mr. Freezes vs. Batman and Robin.

And if you are thinking right now that I'll say, how could it possibly get any worse, forget it. Just forget it.

I'm not biting that hook ever again, no way.

A spell was broken, fortunately, when I pulled Mikie up. First he spun on me in a kind of hostile way. Then his face was there, looking into mine. And, we got it. He all but rapped himself on the head with his knuckles and gave himself a *duh*.

Together we got the rest of it cleaned up. Mikie pulled at Frank, and I grabbed Alex. Without words, Mikie started walking him away down the street. I waved him on, nodding, hurrying him along. He nodded, waved, disappeared.

To leave me sitting on the curb with the man.

"Well, how stupid was that?" I said. Expecting, I guess, exhaustion to bring agreement.

"Very stupid," he said weakly. "And humiliating."

"Right." This was going too well.

"You should have hit him. God, you take a lot of crap off people, Elvin."

"I do not."

"Yes, you do. And your dad wouldn't want that. Your dad would want to know that you were taking care of yourself. That would be important to him. It's important to me. I want to help straighten you out before it's too late."

I thought about it. No, that's too strong. I attempted to think about it. But it was futile. I simply could not manage to relate to what he was telling me, no matter how genuine his intentions were.

"It was just Mikie and Frankie, Alex," I said.

"Ya, and if you can't straighten out those two cream puffs—"

"You weren't exactly mopping up the floor with them yourself, Uncle Alcatraz. You know what I think, I think maybe you were never in prison at all."

It was a joke. See, if I said you had never gone to jail you would see that as a good thing.

His gleaming but scuffed white head dropped into his hands. He stared at the small swatch of ground in between his long, skinny feet, though one of them was mostly shoe. When he spoke it was soft and muffled and cracked so I was forced to lean in to him to hear properly.

"I used to be a lot tougher than that, I swear."

"It's okay," I said quickly, before he cracked open the antidepressants.

"It's not okay."

"You did fine."

"I was a disgrace."

"You were not a . . . well, how do you mean?"

"I used to be tough. I wanted to show you how to be tough. I'm messing up everything now."

"No, no, no, not at all. Listen. All right, I'll tell you, I sort of have been wanting to do that, stand up to those guys, shut them up for a while. Been waiting a long time, in fact. Like, ten years. If it weren't for you, I never would have even done it. It was kind of fun, in the end. Kind of a rush. I just might do it again."

"Now?" He perked up, raised his head, breathed a tiny bit faster.

"Um, maybe later."

"Oh. Okay then."

I put my arm around his shoulders. It felt very weird. Even the sight of my hand on another guy's shoulders looked foreign and peculiar enough to cause me to stare. I couldn't think of another person I had done that to. Mikie? I don't know. Probably. Would figure. Why wouldn't I? But I couldn't recall, or picture, it. Frankie? I'd probably remember. No, not necessarily. Didn't matter. I could do it, could have done it already. But it must have been pretty far from natural since here I was sitting bald and bruised on a curb, and fixated on the sight of my arm around a shoulder of a similarly bald and bruised guy. And he was all grown up.

"Thanks," I said.

He smiled broadly, and no longer looked anything like all grown up.

I got up, stood over him, helped him to his feet. He felt very light, more like opening a door than lifting a whole person.

"I really was a lot tougher before. I swear it."

"Before what?" I asked.

"Before everything. Before your dad died. Before I did stupid things. Before I spent too much time in prison. Before I came out. Before I got sick, then better, then sick again. Before I lost it."

"What do you mean, you lost it? What did you lose?"

Ever see that giveaway move when a person is trying to smile but his face is trying to do something else altogether? When it looks like the bottom lip is pushing up smile style, and his top lip is pushing just as hard against it? It is a very uncomfortable thing to see, don't you think? You'd almost rather see a person break all the way down and scream and babble or something, wouldn't you?

"Alex? Alex? What did you lose?"

He held that expression for an awfully long time. *Held* probably wouldn't even be the right way to put it since he seemed to be held by the face as much as he was holding it. Finally he climbed out of it just enough to speak.

"You want to know. Sure you want to know. You're a good kid, Elvin. My brother's kid of course is a good kid. He would like that. Anyway, you have to know what I lost, since I'm kind of asking you to help me get it back."

There are some times when I think I have regretted every single question I have ever asked.

11

Cool Family

I have always loved trains. If the Wild West could come back without the wildness but with horses and wagons for traffic that would be the best thing, but since it wasn't coming back, trains were definitely the next best thing. I liked the idea of getting on a train, slapping it on the rump, and knowing it was going to know the way. That made me relax, that and the rhythm of trains, the sound of the clack of track, and even the kind of forlorn look of most places that trains seemed to go through anymore.

Alex may have felt the same way, because he closed his eyes just as soon as we took our seats and he snoozed or meditated or just ignored me. Whichever, I was okay with it.

Mostly I was content just to stare. I stared for a good bit out the window at whatever passed, and I stared for a good bit more at my uncle slumped directly across from me in the seat facing mine.

He was even older with his eyes closed. He was very

lined, and very pale. He was smaller. Smaller than me, smaller than himself. Smaller than yesterday. His head shave was grittier than mine, more like coarse sandpaper, and his two noticeable scrape marks were more alive, more ready to weep.

I caught flashes, in my switching views, of my ghosty self in the window, looking not a million miles away from the old Bishop across from me. It was very much like a time-lapse series of photos, as a long row of scrabby pine trees flew past in the background of my face, seeming to move me too far forward, too fast, in the physical sense and in the rotten time sense.

I got a quick shudder for my troubles.

"Would you like to know anything?" Alex's voice asked, making me jolt again. It seemed, with his eyes still closed and his speech slow and faraway, like I was dealing with two complete separate characters, and both a little eerie.

Would I like to know anything? If that were an actual honest question about an actual honest choice, I would have to say no, I would not like to know anything. If you could have no knowledge at all about the past or the present or anything not right in front of you, that would be a simpler, happier thing probably. If you could have *no* knowledge.

But it's never that clean, is it? No, we have to have

mothers and schools and calories behind us that we cannot help but know about, and dead relatives and undead relatives and train conductors coming to ask for tickets anytime now that we can't duck either. So as long as we have to have at least *part* knowledge whether we like it or not, it's probably for the best that we go ahead and take delivery on more information when it is offered to us.

"I would like to know, from an experienced, Bishop point of view, what is the scariest part of growing older?"

That opened his eyes. He sat upright and rubbed weariness from his temples and forehead.

"Well, I sort of meant did you want to know anything about the family, before you meet them. But, fair enough, the question was rather open-ended. The answer is nose hair."

I waited.

The conductor came and took our tickets. Alex stared after him as if they were going to have to have a duel. Nose hairs at dawn.

"Nose hairs aren't scary, Alex."

He smiled. "One day about twenty-five years from now, you're gonna look close in a mirror and you're gonna want to cry. Remember your ol' Uncle Alex that day, okay, boy?"

I shrugged and nodded.

"They are your cousins, Elvin. The kids you're going to see. Can you appreciate that?"

"I cannot, no."

"The boy works out, I understand. Like you do."

"About that. I've been thinking, working out kind of hurts. My muscles are still aching me, and that's supposed to be gone by now, I should think. So I'm thinking instead, rather than work out, maybe I'll just let myself go."

"Let yourself go? You mean this is you holding on?"

"Good one."

"You like it?"

"No."

Alex laughed like a kindly old man. Then he lifted up his shirt and produced a tall rectangular bottle from the waist of his pants. Tequila. He took a drink. "Here, try it," he said. "Two buddies on a train with a bottle between them. It's a special thing. A religious thing, really. Found this before I found Jesus, to be honest. Me and my brother had this thing. Now me and his boy have it."

Alex was smiling so hard through that last bit it looked like his old face might tear open. I wanted to reach across and pat his cheeks down smooth to keep them together.

Instead, I reached and took the bottle.

"So now I have to keep up with Jesus and my dad, huh?"

"Big shoes all around, Elvin Bishop. Big, big shoes."

"Is this stuff going to give you another seizure?"

"Nah. As long as I stay away from the too-sweet stuff, I'm okay."

From what I understood, tequila did not fall into the category of too-sweet stuff. I leaned back and took my first-ever swallow of Mexico's famous elixir.

And nearly filled my big, big shoes with big, big puke. I had been well informed on the lack of sweetness.

But I held it mightily together. I gagged a bit, half swallowed, brought it back up again, choked it back down, almost, then, for good.

"Ahhh," I said loudly, that sound that could stand for refreshment or thank-God-that's-over.

I had met the world's worst flavor.

"I know, fine, isn't it?" Alex asked as he took the bottle back.

He took another sip and then as we talked the bottle passed back between us. He sipped, passed, talked. I held the bottle politely, passed it back, talked. If he noticed I wasn't drinking, he wasn't saying.

Not that I needed to drink it. The first sip, fumes, and memories kept me spinning.

"Are they like me in any other ways?" I asked him about his kids.

"Your father was pretty self-absorbed too, you know that. But in a good way. In a funny way, like yourself."

Did I ask that? Oh, wait, now I see it. I guess I did.

"But the kids, Alex? What are they like?"

He went into that scary, fractured grimace smile. I hated that. He took his drink, then he took mine as I sat with my hand outstretched. I was only doing it to break his pace anyway.

"I don't really know," he said.

"How come?" I said.

"Because. Of a combination of stuff. Because of mothers, and courts. And themselves."

I let it hang, and I almost let him drink, then suddenly some other part of myself, some bossier, more together part of myself, snagged the bottle away.

"That's why you don't know your children, Alex? Those are the reasons?"

He was staring out the window now. It was the ugliest stuff; you wouldn't want to stare at it. Thrown-away tires held his eye like they were talking to him.

"But you like me, don't you, son?" he said, staring out the window still at the word *but*, but staring at me by the time he got to *son*. "You are a fine kid, and you like ol' Alex, don't you?"

"I like you, Alex."

"I mean, I cooked for you, right? Cooked very well. I give you advice. I tell you stuff and show you stuff you ought to know, right? I let you in on Jesus and working out and saunas, but just enough and not too much, right? I fill you in on Thai food and Dead Bishops. I brought you your horn. We jammed, right? Told you not to worry about your penis, too. I fought for you. We fought together, remember that?"

Was it an effort to recall something that happened that same afternoon? Maybe. These were long days, these days.

"I remember, Alex."

"And when you got your ugly hair off, who was right alongside you to get his own ugly hair off?"

"That was you, Alex."

"Damn right it was me. We've had some times, you and me, haven't we?"

"Technically it's probably not plural, since really it's more like one big, long time we're having this week . . . but yes, we've had one, all right."

"We have. And I found out you're a good kid. Through it all. Even if you're a little soft—that'll pass— and a little goofy sometimes, you are a good, good kid. I found out my brother's boy is a good, good kid. And you found out I was a good man, am I right? That your dad's brother is a good man, ya?"

It was in the way he had to ask. It was in the fragile high note he hit when he asked that *ya?*

"It's all true, Alex. You're a good man."

He went quiet, a steely quiet rather than a mopey one, which was good. He looked back out the window.

"Good, then. Very good. If you can like me, and I can be a good man with a good kid like you . . . then there's something to me. There is something to me, and that will show. Thank you. Thank you very much, Elvin."

I always thought having some power, any kind of power, would be an unquestionably good thing. I never had any that I was aware of, always wanted some, even a little taste.

This tasted like it was it. It was not an unquestionably good taste.

"You're welcome, Uncle Alex."

"Press the buzzer, Elvin."

"You press the buzzer. At least they know you."

"That's my problem. Press the buzzer and I'll wait around the side of the house."

"How 'bout I press the buzzer and we both wait around the side of the house?"

"You know what's incredible?"

"I can think of a number of things. You mean incredible

in the whole world sense of things or incredible as in right here right now in front of this door? Either way, I can think of a number—"

"What is incredible is that I came around in the first place to show you how to behave more like me, and here you've got me acting just like you. You are like some kind of powerful force for God knows what, Elvin Bishop."

"You're welcome," I said.

"That was not a thank-you; it was a confession."

"Oh right. Then as long as we are here, skulking and cowering, etcetera, are there any other timely confessions you should make regarding this buzzer and why it isn't being rung?"

The door by then had run out of patience and threw itself open. Perhaps with some assistance.

"What are you doing on my doorstep, you awful, awful man?"

Ah, a turn for the better.

"Hiya, Mags," Alex said, truly excited to see a person who appeared to want to spit on him.

"Hiya nothing. What are you after?"

"I'm not after anything. I just thought . . . I just came . . . just thought it was time and all . . . this is your nephew, Elvin."

He said that part, after the stumbling mumbling part, as if it were a momentous, big, warm deal to all parties.

He may have misfigured.

"Elvin," he continued, "this is your aunt, Mags the Lady."

She paused, just long enough to build up some more steamy bile and to let out a threatening sigh.

"Hello, Elvis. But sorry, you are not related to me. You were sort of related at one time, by marriage, because I was married to this rat here, who was brothers with the other rat—sorry, kid—who was related to you. But since I am no longer related in any way to this rat here—thank God—and the other rat is no longer with us—sorry, and thank God—you and me, Elvis, pal, are released from those particular chains of bondage. Do say hi to your mother for me, though."

I just kept blinking. My eyeballs were all dried out from the blast of her hostility, and I felt as if my lashes had been melted off, finally completing the morbid transforming of Alex and me into the same atrocity.

"Okay," I said meekly, "I'll tell her."

I turned and started walking away, back toward the train station, away from here and from this and from Alex and toward home, toward my mother and my life and a long sleep to wipe it all away.

"What is that?" came a new voice at my back.

"That, I'm afraid, is your cousin, Elvis."

I stopped. Curiosity grabbed and turned me, and I

returned to the gathering. There, along with Alex and his ex, was a kid. About my height, my age, my coloring. He was a bit thinner than me, but bulky anyway, athletic in a footbally way.

I stopped at my usual spot, on the doorstep, and I stared at him. He stared at me.

"I heard about you," he said with a hard, flat grin.

"I hadn't heard about you," I said.

"What happened to your head?"

"See," Alex cut in, "look how the boys are getting along already. Peas in a pod."

Then, behind the boy, a girl appeared. She was probably a year older. She looked nothing like any of us. She was tall and thin, had long, tea-colored hair and melon-colored eyes and cheeks that clearly had bones in them.

"Oh God," she said, looking back and forth between me and Alex, "would you get them in off the step before somebody sees them."

"Yes," Alex piped, "get us off your step before somebody sees us."

The two kids backed into the house. Mags the Lady didn't budge. Alex, assuming the best, had started on in, then froze at her resistance.

"Look like crap," she said to him.

"Feel like crap," he said brightly.

"*Are* crap," the two voices chimed from inside.

Slowly Mags the Lady relented, backing away through the front door, letting us follow along just so, like a lion tamer with a whip and a chair.

It got a lot more comfortable once we got inside. We were not invited to sit down; rather the whole crowd of us stood in the borderland that lay between the kitchen and the living/dining area, the only thing differentiating the two being the different tartan patterns of the carpet tiling.

"Hey," I said, breaking the tension, "my dog got beat up by a dog wearing a little rain jacket that was almost the exact pattern as your floor. Huh. Small world."

"Isn't it, though," the girl cousin drawled in such a way that I didn't think she was considering my dog story at all. "And stop staring at me, you."

I was not staring at her. I mean, if you were going to stare at anybody in this room, it would be her without question, but I wasn't.

"Ma, the fat guy is staring at me."

"Swan, don't be unkind. His name is Elvis."

Swan. Wow. That was a name. What a name that was. Swan. And it fit, too, because this girl was a Swan if ever there was one. Amazing how people's names fit who they are.

"Hey, ah, *Elvis*," Alex said, "are you going to correct people as to your real name, or are you just going to change it officially so as not to bother anybody?"

"Sorry."

"Stop apologizing. It's your name, for pete's sake."

"It's Elvin, actually. Though it's a common mistake, the Elvis thing."

"Not the young Elvis, that's for sure," Swan said. "Maybe the old, crazy, fat, dead one. Though even he wasn't all bald and scabby."

"That is some mouth on that girl of yours, Mags. Nobody ever taught you any manners, Swan?" Alex said.

Swan was no more intimidated by him than she was by me. "Why are you here, anyway? Why don't you go haunt one of your other families, you old spook? You old skin-headed zombie."

Even before she said the zombie thing, I felt as if I were in *The Mummy* or something. Like I had stumbled into some old cave full of secrets and stories and spooky stuff I didn't want to know about and wasn't supposed to know about and would probably pay some awful price for knowing about. His other families? There were too many families popping up already, thanks. I didn't want there to be any more.

"Elvis, you want to go see my stuff?" the boy said. "We can leave all them to have it out."

"Hawk, I want you to stay," Alex said, almost like pleading.

Hawk. There's another one. How cool was that? What a cool family they must have been back when.

Maybe we were cool families back then. Maybe, before things all went all wrong, we were something great, this Bishop dynasty. Maybe maybe. Wish I knew. Wish I remembered. Wish it was, and still was.

Hawk laughed, but it wasn't really a laugh, you know?

"That's very funny. Can you say that again? *I want you to stay.* That's very funny."

Alex did not say it again.

"Elvis, you coming to see my stuff?"

Hawk walked down the hall, and I looked to Alex. He nodded with a kind of a quarter of a smile. Maybe that was how much of him wanted me to go down the hall with Hawk, while the other three-quarters wanted us all in the same room.

When I got to the end of the hall to the open door, Hawk was waiting for me. Standing amidst his room and his possessions like it was a showroom where he was selling things, or a game show set where I could win any of these fabulous prizes.

This was his stuff.

"How do you like my stuff?" he asked.

There was something in the way he said the word *stuff*, with extra emphasis, that worried me.

"Nice stuff," I said, shrugging.

"Ya, it is," he said. "Good *stuff*. It's my *stuff*."

He brushed past me, jumped up to grab the chin-up bar mounted in his door frame. He chinned himself up. I counted. He did twenty of them. Then he dropped back down.

"Want to do some chin-ups?"

"Oh," I said and as my mind scrambled through my vast back catalogue of physical excuses, I perked up at the realization of a real one. And a pretty cool-sounding one to boot. "Can't." I rubbed my left biceps and shoulder with my right hand, then did that sort of stretching motion that looks like you are trying to fly by using your elbows for wings, "I was working out . . . earlier already . . . muscles a little sore right now." Okay, *earlier* was stretching things, but they were sore.

"Oh," Hawk said, nodding in a completely skeptical, underimpressed way. "Well, then, want to see the rest of my *stuff*?" He slammed the door.

I had gotten a little too wrapped up in my own workout excuse because then I went back to rubbing my biceps, checking for signs of life, signs of life being pain, of course, like they always are.

And while my head was down and my response time was slow, Hawk decided to take the situation in hand.

That is, he decided to take me in hand. Or in arm.

He grabbed me right around the head and squeezed so

hard I thought orange juice might come out.

"Hey," I shouted.

"Here, come here, let me show you my *stuff*," he said, dragging me by the head over to his large set of chrome hand weights stacked neatly on their own rack. "These are my dumbbells. Maybe you know each other, you have a lot in common. Dumbbells, this is Elvis; Elvis, these are the dumbbells." As he said this, Hawk raised and lowered my head with a vicious jerking motion, like I was nodding violently to his weights.

"And over here," he said, dragging me to the opposite corner of the room, "is SlamMan." SlamMan was a human-shaped form of molded plastic and foam padding set on a wide base. He had a series of what looked like reflectors in his eyes, mouth, and at various spots on his upper body. "He is the greatest boxing trainer."

Hawk continued to hold me firmly in the grip of one powerful arm while gesturing at SlamMan with his free hand. "When I press this button"—he pressed—"the lights blink in random sequence." The lights all over SlamMan did begin to blink in a sequence that appeared to be random. With each blink there was an accompanying high-pitched beep, not unlike the one coming from me every couple of seconds. "Then I have to try and hit the targets. It's great *stuff*. Say hi to SlamMan, Elvis."

I myself was never much for those line-in-the-sand-type moments. I always figured, you start drawing those lines in that sand, then people are going to start crossing them and very likely make things uncomfortable on your side of the line. Whereas if you hadn't drawn attention to your side by drawing that line in the first place, they probably wouldn't even have bothered.

But even I had to have limits of some kind. Even I, with my highly practical view of what is and is not worth getting worked up about, had to acknowledge that there were some depths to which I must refuse to sink or else risk ever more imaginative levels of degradation farther down.

Against my own better judgment, I had to make this a line-in-the-sand moment.

"I will not be saying hi to SlamMan."

The pause at this moment was more painful than the headlock. Even though he had added a kind of sand-papery grinding motion to it.

"Ouch," I said, though I knew it was unlikely to change his opinion. My back was starting to hurt from being bent over. And leaned on.

"What has SlamMan ever done to you?" Hawk said in a big, sad voice, while SlamMan beeped innocently in the background.

"I see what you're doing. You are going to try and make me talk about SlamMan like he's an actual person, and make me look stupid anyway. Well, I'm not falling for it," I said into his forearm.

"Good point," Hawk said. "You don't want to look stupid. Here, we'll just work out with him then." As he said that, he rushed me forward, ramming me hard into SlamMan's well-toned abs. Then he rammed me again. Then again, and I was starting to see the pattern. I was following the sequence of flashing lights—and even adding some of my own—as Hawk mashed me again and again into the wall of SlamMan.

He was talking to me while he did this, while he smacked me silly, while I struggled lamely. He was talking, then kind of moaning, then kind of growling, then back to talking again. SlamMan kept beeping like a shy electro soundtrack to our own little gangster movie.

"So what are you, his kid now?" Hawk said. "You his kid? That's great. That's great."

Every time he said something, he had to whack my head. It hurt more and more, and the humiliation of not being able to do anything about it was making me have the totally perverse and desperate reaction of praying that Alex would not come in and see this.

"Well, that's just great," Hawk said. "So you just take him, the two of you just take each other, and get the hell out of my house. Get out of my house. This is my house and this is my *stuff*, and nobody needs you here and nobody wants you here. I am the man here. Not you, not him. I am the man here."

At the end of his program, SlamMan let out one last, long beep and held it for about five seconds. That was Hawk's cue to stop the ramming and give me one last definitive heave-ho, sending me sailing headlong into SlamMan, hitting him, wobbling him, caroming off and continuing past, into the corner, into the wall, onto the floor.

I was stunned as much as anything. Not true. I was hurt more than anything, then embarrassed, then scared. But beyond that, as much as anything, I was stunned.

"All I wanted was to meet you," I said as I slowly got to my feet.

"Ya? How would your ass like to meet my foot?"

It was right about here I lost faith in our ability to work this out.

"Well, my ass is very busy so it won't be meeting any new body parts this week." I walked across the room, past Hawk, who was heavy-breathing and alarmingly seeming to be getting still angrier. But he let me pass without further incident. My head, still new from the razor, felt red raw as I rubbed my hand over it.

"I mean it," Hawk said as I opened the bedroom door. "If I see either one of you again, you'll be sorry."

"I believe you," I said. "I'm already sorry."

He rushed up and slammed the door behind me.

I walked the long hallway back toward the living room with something like dread filling me. All the time I was in playing with Hawk and his *stuff*, my mind was—understandably, I'd say—distracted from the main business of Alex and what he was doing in this place, with these people.

There was a deeply unsettling silence waiting like dead air as I reached the end of the hallway. Back at the other end, I heard SlamMan start to beep again, then Hawk banging on him with two ferocious fists. Or possibly one ferocious baseball bat.

I crept, like a burglar. Don't know why. There was no need. Nobody was looking for me, or looking out for me, or especially concerned with me. But it was like I felt I could escape, like I could avoid something I didn't want to encounter here, just as long as I was good and quiet.

Well I couldn't. When I got to that spot where I had left them before, where the kitchen area turned into the living area because the bluish tartan turned into the reddish tartan, I found the scene. Not the scene I left, actually, but a warped and melted version of it more brutal and sad than the dance with Cousin Hawk.

Swan was nowhere to be seen. Mags the Lady was there, leaning with her back against the scabby Formica top of the kitchen counter, her arms folded tightly, and a snarl on her face that showed all her teeth all the way back to the joints of her jaws.

On the floor in front of her, spread on the bluish tartan floor in front of her, was Alex. He was on his haunches, back hunched, palms and face flat to the floor. You could hear nothing other than a sniff every couple of seconds.

Mags the Lady looked at me when I walked in. Her body remained planted as a tree, but her head turned, her neck flexing one side like a racehorse. She held that pose good and long, and just stared at me, stared like she needed to look through my eyes and read the fine print written on the back wall of the inside of my skull.

Then she turned away again.

"I don't even care whether it is true or not," she said to Alex's back. "I don't care. I will never care. The kids don't care. Nobody cares; nobody will ever care. And nobody wants anything from you."

He just laid there. Motionless, but for the sniffing.

Mags the Lady turned in her powerful, horsey style once more. "This is your one chance to take him out of here before the police do it, Elvis."

She didn't have to say it twice. I went right over to my uncle and lifted him up off the floor. He was damp and floppy and insubstantial as a bath towel. I kept one arm around him and steered him toward out. He didn't struggle or complain or express anything at all. It was like she beat him up, and beat him badly.

"How can you people be so mean?" I said as we walked out the front door.

"Yes," said Mags the Lady, "how can we? Do say hello to your mother for me, though."

Then she shut the door crisply behind us.

12

Ouch

Tomorrow came, as so far it has always done. I didn't expect to see Alex that day, or the day after that. The day after that, though, I allowed myself to think, maybe. Chump.

By Friday, I had no expectations. No expectations is a sound way to start any day, I think. And by Saturday, I was pretty well clean of any *memory* of any expectations.

She was sitting on the couch, sipping tea when I came down. She had mail in her lap.

My mother was wearing sweatpants. My world had no order at all anymore.

I sat down next to her.

"You planning to go on a daytime talk show today?" I said, eyeing up her outfit.

"I thought I'd be prepared," she said coolly, "in case any called. You never know."

I couldn't help thinking this was not a legitimate explanation.

"My mother is wearing sweatpants," I said more urgently.

She giggled. She liked it when seemingly small things unsettled me.

"Where is Uncle Alex?" I finally, finally asked.

She neatly slipped a letter at me out of the stack like she was dealing me a card. It was in a gray envelope, with overly proud lettering stamped on it. It was a sniffy-looking letter.

I picked it up. It was scented with French onion soup. Gourmet, but rank. Before I could make the effort of reading, she paraphrased for me.

"It's from Alex. He says he died in a plane crash. Again."

I didn't say anything. I read the letter. The letter didn't say anything either. Damn rotten letter.

She took a sip, and a sigh, and leaned in to me.

"I liked him," I said after a very long wait.

I took her cup, and a sip.

"I know," she said.

"I mean, what's the deal, Ma? He comes here when I don't want him. He hangs around when I don't want him. Then, when he makes me want him, he's gone."

She squeezed my shoulder. "That, in a nutshell, is men, Elvin Bishop."

"Well, *I'll* never be one, I can promise you that." I

took another sip of tea. I could sense Grog out there on the periphery, waiting for that delectable tea bag.

"Okay," she said, and looked at me with that look. I wondered where she ever got her complete understanding of everything. I marveled at it, and I feared it. And if I thought about it too hard, I could probably work out how she acquired it, so I wouldn't be thinking about it too hard.

"Or maybe it's you," I said. "This appears to be the third time you have lost a full-grown Bishop."

First she made a startled face. Then she made like she was counting on her fingers. "You know, I think you're right. I must be bad for their health."

Sometimes even our jokes made me nervous.

"Should I be worried?" I asked, inviting her motherly reassurance.

"Probably," she said.

And because she was *my* mother and not yours, that was reassurance.

"Ah well," I said. "What're you gonna do?"

She shrugged. "Go to the gym? Start taking care of ourselves?"

"Sure. We can go to the gym. I was thinking I wanted to do more of that. Exercise. Watch my appetites. Watch my sugar. Maybe get a little tougher. Keep healthy heart and toes and stuff. You do have to take care of yourself, you know?"

"You do. You have to take care of yourself."

And if you take care of yourself, what do you get? Do you get to keep your toes and your physique and your family? Do you get golden curls and great posture and unlimited love and adoration?

I never saw my mother in sweatpants before that morning.

I never saw Mikie eat a vegetable.

I never saw Frankie wash his hands in a public bathroom. Though he may have just forgotten by the time he finished with everything else.

I never once saw my dog take a drink of water beyond what she squeezed out of teabags.

I handed Ma back her cup and stood to look at myself in the mirror opposite over the mantle. It was an ancient thing, that mirror, sideways oval, smokey and chipped with age, bordered in a kind of vine-carved frame with twelve coats of cream paint on it. Ma popped up next to me. We looked like a weird 1880s prairie couple.

I could swear my neck already looked a little bigger, and my face a little smaller. I was bald, and my head had small cuts on it. I thought I could make out the beginnings of creases in my forehead. A completely different guy from a couple of weeks ago. Who was that guy?

"You know," Ma said with a big, satisfied smile, "you never change."

I gave her a nice smile right back. "I know. And why would I want to? By the way, Mags the Lady says hi," I said.

The old prairie couple just stared at us.

"Holy smokes," she said. Said it beautifully, I thought.

"Right, Mother, we're going to the gym," I said, heading upstairs to get my gear.

My gear. I still had to shake my head.

But you have to try, don't you. You have to take care of yourself, even if taking care of yourself is not what you're wired for, because you do have something to say about it all.

And because it probably matters to somebody. You never know.

Take care of yourself, then.